Force
of
Habit

Also by Marian Allen

Novels

SAGE Book 1: The Fall of Onagros
SAGE Book 2: Bargain With Fate
SAGE Book 3: Silver and Iron
Sideshow in the Center Ring
A Dead Guy at the Summerhouse
The Wolves of Port Novo
(Previously Published as Eel's Reverence)
Bar Sinister

Short Story Collections

Lonnie, Me and. . . .
Lonnie, Me and the Hound of Hell
Turtle Feathers
The King of Cherokee Creek
MA's Monthly Hot Flashes: 2002-2009
Other Earth, Other Stars
Shifty
Frenemies in Space

Force of Habit

of

Habit

Marian Allen

Per Bastet

Force of Habit

Published by Per Bastet Publications LLC, P.O. Box 3023
Corydon, IN 47112

Cover art by Ciera Blane Art

ISBN 978-1-942166-94-8

Available in trade paperback and DRM-free ebook formats

Force
of
Habit

Dedication

For my husband, Charles, who loved me in spite of the occasional miscommunication; for Devra Langsam, who encouraged me (blame her); and for Jane Peyton, who let the character of Tetra come over and play.

Chapter 1

On the planet Llannonn, a man and a woman faced one another over a battered computer desk-panel in the office of Jok'rel's Traveler's Rest Inn.

Each held a thick glass of clear liquid. The woman clutched hers so tightly her knuckles showed red against her whitened fingers.

She, a native of the planet, might have been a nondescript human: medium-brown hair, medium-brown eyes, medium-brown skin, Earthling-average height, weight, build.

The man lounged in an upholstered swivel chair, picking loose threads from its fabric with the air of a man making a social call.

But Gord Pron wasn't making a social call. His lemon-yellow skin, emerald hair, beady black eyes, and lack of lips proclaimed his origin. He was a Stokk, and he meant business.

"I have a speculation to put before you, Bookkeeper Freldt Saymak," Gord Pron said, his parted mouth-rim showing his teeth in a charmless smile. He spoke in Allesesperanto, a hybrid Intergalactic language, serviceable for trade, diplomacy, and criminal rhetoric. "Suppose you had a friend who wanted to take over this, oh," the Stokk pretended to search for a random example, "this inn franchise. A Traveler's Rest Inn, like Jok'rel's, here. And suppose the man who had the franchise wouldn't transfer it. What would you do?"

"I'd tell my friend to want something else."

The Stokk laughed. "But suppose your friend was set on the idea. I mean, really set on it. Suppose he was so set on it, you thought somebody might get sick over it. Maybe fall down and crack his head or something. You'd want to help your friend, wouldn't you?"

"Yes," Freldt said, "I'd want to help my friend."

"Sure, you would. You're smart. You have to be smart, to be a bookkeeper. If you made a mistake with the books, you could ruin a place, couldn't you? An eent here, a biht there; it all adds up, eh? 'Take care of the luhmps, and the krelps will take care of themselves,' eh?"

The woman said nothing.

Gord Pron's beady black eyes glinted, and his lips would have thinned, if he had had any. "You must not have heard me. I asked you a question. I said, you could ruin a place, couldn't you?"

Freldt's jaw slackened, then snapped tight. "*You're* the one who started the rumor we make our mishmash out of alley jammers," she said. "And you're the one who laid false information against us with the Cleanliness Bureau. And you called that trashy newscast and had it report how many times the Inspectors had been in, but not how they'd cleared us every time."

"I don't like to brag."

"Why don't you just keep it up? Business has been falling off; all you have to do is wait."

"'Slow but steady wins the tontine,'" the man agreed. "But a business with a bad reputation isn't really a good business to take over, is it? Besides, we're talking about *you*, remember? You and good old Knosh Jok'rel, and how you'd like to help him? Like you say, he's been having a lot of problems lately, and it's probably getting him down. The Inn is maybe getting to be too much for him, but he just doesn't want to admit it. You'd be doing him a favor to help him get out, while he still has his health."

"I see," said Freldt.

"Sure, you do. Like I said, you're smart. And you've got a good heart. Such kindness should not go unrewarded, if you know what I mean. My friend likes your friend. If you take care of your friend, my friend will take care of you. Otherwise, my friend will take care of both of you. Get it?"

"Got it."

"Good." Gord Pron nodded. "Now, we don't want to rush you," he said. "Think it over. I'll meet you in the bar here, say, at fourteen hundred hours on Sixday, to see what you decide. Until then, let's just keep our good deed to ourselves, shall we?"

He tossed off his drink and left a very worried bookkeeper in his wake.

~*~

Meanwhile, aboard the Galactic Union Spaceship *St. Gregory the Wonderworker*, a woman mused darkly.

Three more years. I shall run mad.

Isobel Enid Schuster almost wished there had been no Vatican IV, and the clergy had not gone co-ed, or at least the Jesuits had not. Then, St. Bennedetta's would never have been founded, she would never have attended, and the Board would never have given her hiring preference as an Old Girl. If she hadn't been hired as a teacher at St. Bennedetta's, she'd still be on Earth. Dear old Earth. . . .

"We're transferring you," Mother Hadrian had said. "You're aware of the training vessel we operate in conjunction with the Galactic Union Space Troopers? *St. Gregory The Wonderworker?*"

"The one the kids call the *Uncle Gus*? Yes." She had snorted a little. She remembered clearly having snorted, filled with contemptuous pity for the poor suckers assigned to that high-tech armpit.

"You have a challenging and rewarding. . . ," Mother Hadrian referred to Bel's contract, "five years ahead of you in the marvel of outer space. Go with God."

So here she was, stuck on *Uncle Gus* for another three years, facing another uphill climb in Extra-Terrestrial Humanities and

Value Systems 101.

If only she could get away, just for a while. The strain of behaving like a responsible adult twenty-four hours a day was wearing. That's what it was: It was wearing.

~*~

Also aboard the *Uncle Gus*, two humanoid amphibians from the planet Gilhoo left the teachers' mail room and turned into the corridor.

Tetra and Quatro Petrie had been spawned in the same dish, ripened in the same incubator, and reared in the same household. Both were pale, and both had gills on either side of their necks, but there the resemblance ended.

Tetra had thick black hair in short loose curls. Never more than a dusting of black fuzz covered Quatro's skull, like the plush on a cheap toy; now, as usual, he capped his head with an ill-fitting wig. Tetra was petite and nicely padded. Quatro was tall and thin, like a walking test tube.

Tetra had a theory about their differences: "Our genetic inheritance is uneven. He got the height and I got the personality."

As they reached Isobel Schuster's classroom, next to Tetra's, two down from his own, Quatro said, "Don't forget Ven Schuster's envelope."

"I have not forgotten. I am not in the habit of forgetting things."

Tetra never used contractions. She had noted, during her civil service term with the Intergalactic Red Starburst emergency aid organization, that Earthlings never questioned the integrity of people who didn't use contractions. It had been difficult to get the hang of, but it had come in very handy from time to time.

Ven Schuster slouched in her Floatachair as if one of her students had flipped her Off switch on the way out.

Tetra regarded her. *Frumpy looking little thing.* (Bel was six inches taller than the Gilhoolie woman, but Tetra tended

4

to think of everyone else as smaller than herself.) Brown hair, brown eyes, brown skin, brown suit. *She looks like a mud puddle with buttons.*

But looks can be deceiving. Bel had a reputation as a troublemaker. Tetra liked that in a person.

"Ven Schuster," Tetra said, calling Bel out of her reverie.

Bel looked up. Looked over, rather, for Bel set her Floatachair high, and Tetra stood at Bel's sitting eye level. When the new students short-sheeted the faculty's beds (which they traditionally did, the first night out of port), Tetra never noticed.

So, Bel looked over. "Yes, Ven Petrie? Is this some kind of inter-departmental meeting? Am I supposed to know about it?"

"I just stopped by to give you this." Tetra handed Bel an envelope. "From the Captain."

"Probably more rules and regs, or Q's and A's, or some other official-type time waster." Bel tossed it on her desk.

"I would read it, if I were you," Tetra said. "Otherwise, how will you know what to defy?"

With an exaggeration that spoke of hours of cartoon viewing and practice before a mirror, Tetra opened her mouth and closed one eye in a wink as broad as the known universe.

Chapter 2

Freldt watched out the window until the Stokk took off in his luxury hovercar, then put in a visicall to Pel Darzin, the District Criminal Investigator of the Meadow of Flowers District of Council City.

Pel Darzin sat at the desk, directly before the camera. He wasn't quite pudgy, but he trembled on the verge. He had high, rounded cheekbones, bright with youthful vigor. His fine black hair was parted just above his left ear and combed over, in the official constabulary style. Had Freldt but known it, he looked very much like a young Peter Lorre.

"I apologize," he said, "but my visiscreen needs calibrating again. All I can see of you is a sort of brown blur, like a mud puddle with buttons. Oh, I do beg your pardon. I meant no offense."

"None taken," said Freldt, "but thank you for your courtesy."

That social gaffe navigated, Darzin returned to business. "Please identify yourself verbally."

"Bookkeeper Freldt Saymak, resident of this city."

"Yes, Bookkeeper Freldt Saymak," he said. "May I help you?"

Freldt had a sudden attack of Second Thoughts. A well-ordered society stays well-ordered by developing a strong law-giving structure, backed up with a no-nonsense body of implementers. In other words, mouth and muscle. Any brain involved was strictly by the way. Freldt asked herself if she really wanted to throw herself into the arms of the law, where she would be as likely to find a billy-club as a Good Citizenship Medal.

She decided to test the attitudinal waters. "My employer, Innkeeper Knosh Jok'rel, has been threatened, through me, by a Stokk named Gord Pron."

"We are familiar with the Stokk Gord Pron," said Darzin. "He's an enforcer for a Stokk Innkeeper named Boktu Jippir."

"But Innkeeper Knosh Jok'rel knows Stokk Innkeeper Boktu Jippir. Socially, I mean. They drink in each other's bars, eat in each other's restaurants. The Stokk Gord Pron indicated today that his employer would go to any lengths to drive Innkeeper Knosh Jok'rel out of business."

"And?"

"Stokk Innkeeper Boktu Jippir is already a wealthy man. Why would he need another Inn? Why would he be willing to destroy a friend to get what he doesn't need?"

Pel Darzin turned a hand palm-up. "Off-worlders," he said. "Take this fellow, What's-His-Name, the one who's been working the bars. Well, that's another case. Do you have any proof of the Stokk's threat, or of his employer's involvement?"

Freldt hemmed and hawed but was forced to admit, "No."

"Is there anything else?"

"Yes. The Stokk Gord Pron told me he's been spreading those unappetizing rumors about our restaurant and laid false information against us with the Cleanliness Bureau."

"He confessed?"

"I accused him, and he admitted it."

Pel Darzin began typing. "Exact words?"

"Let me think. He said, 'I don't like to brag.' I accused him and he said, 'I don't like to brag.'"

"Not, 'Yes, I did those things,' or 'You've got me dead to rights,' or 'Let's see you do something about it, Sister'?"

"No."

Darzin pushed a button which looked, from the visiphone camera's angle, as if it said, "Delete."

"Bookkeeper Freldt Saymak, would you like to tell me what the Stokk Gord Pron wanted with you?"

Time to fish or cut bait. "He wanted to bribe me to cook our books," Freldt said.

"And," Darzin said, in the tone of a stern yet compassionate parent to a possibly repentant child, "would you like to tell me whether or not you agreed?"

"I did not agree," said Freldt. "I equivocated."

"Well done," said the officer. "I hoped you hadn't called to confess."

"No, I called to inform. The Stokk Gord Pron wants me to meet him Sixday to give him my answer. In the Traveler's Rest Inn bar, at fourteen hundred hours."

Darzin's thick, agile hands hesitated over his keypad. "Would it do me any good to take a statement?"

Freldt reviewed her conversation with the Stokk enforcer. "No," she said.

Darzin displayed the kind of thought that had caused him to zoom up through the ranks like a glass of prune juice in reverse. "If you could lead him to repeat his threats, and if I or one of my people could hear, we'd have something to use in court. We'd like to make an example of one or two of these Stokk villains. They're becoming as impertinent as alley jammers."

"This one certainly is," said Freldt. "Why is it permitted? What is our Council thinking of, allowing it?"

Darzin leaned closer to the sound sensor and murmured, "Bookkeeper Freldt Saymak, have you reported this to any other authority? Did you call the Grand Council before you called me?"

"No."

"Good. Bookkeeper Freldt Saymak, please keep this to yourself, but I believe one of the Council is working with Stokk Innkeeper Boktu Jippir."

Freldt said nothing. Shock sometimes had that effect on her.

"Meet Stokk Gord Pron on Sixday, as agreed," said Pel Darzin. "How will I or another Investigator recognize you?"

"I'll wear a lilac double-breasted jumpsuit with a plaid peplum, and I'll be playing Solitary Coup d'Etat."

"Solitary Coup d'Etat, eh? Impressive! Well, we'll be in touch, then, on Sixday, if not before."

Freldt Saymak, with the child-like faith of the born accountant (who maintains, in the face of all evidence to the contrary, that figures don't lie), broke the phone connection.

She, like Darzin, saw the difficulty of pinning down a pair of Stokk and a crooked Councilor. She also realized that, while failure might lead to the termination of Darzin's career, she'd face termination of a different and more drastic sort at the hands of Pron and his employer.

It would be all right, she told herself. Wouldn't it be all right? *Please, let it be all right.*

~*~

District Criminal Investigator Pel Darzin hoped he had left his caller more confident than she had any reasonable right to feel.

He allowed himself to assume Bookkeeper Freldt Saymak could get a Stokk to make a direct threat. He further allowed himself to assume he or someone he could trust would be able to bear witness.

He couldn't assume it would lead to a conviction, or even that he'd still be on the force when the dust settled. If the rogue Councilor should get wind of the investigation and stop it or turn it against him, what could he do? What could he do against a member of the Grand Council?

Devious methods seemed called for, and Darzin doubted he'd find his limited circuitousness sufficient to his need.

~*~

Tetra entered her classroom and the door closed behind her.

The intercom ting-ed first call to second period. No one would arrive until just before the last call; she had time to read her own copy of the Captain's directive.

A pass. A "liberty." A "shore leave," the Captain called it. *On Llannonn?*

Interesting. Llannonn wasn't part of the Galactic Union, although the Union, for reasons known best to itself, was wooing the planet.

Funny way to woo: foisting us onto an unsuspecting populace.

It might even be worth going. It would be the first liberty she'd taken since she and Quatro had come aboard five years ago. Perhaps, away from the tedium and trivia of the commonplace, an otherwise unlikely chumship would develop with someone or other. Tetra had many acquaintances, but, alas, no chums.

She accessed the mainframe and accepted leave.

Abuzz with possibilities, she began covering the boardwall with conjugations of irregular Vestigian verbs for the coming Linguistics Honors class. Through the bulkhead between the classrooms, she heard Ven Schuster singing something about being off on the road to somewhere.

Chapter 3

Bel spent three days reading up on Llannonn. Actually, she spent most of the time trying to find something to read; although Llannonn had been under study for some time, she found only the most general information. This, Bel read.

Thank you, Sweet Little Baby Jesus, for the subscription to Infodumps R Us my Granny Ellen gave me for Christmas.

There were three distinct sociotypes on Llannonn: the Urbans, who lived in the towns and cities; the Rurals, who lived in the villages and countryside; and the Wanderers, sometimes known as the Wandering Tribes, who lived wherever they damned well pleased.

The planet's governing body was the Grand Council, made up of two members of each sociotype.

The day before shore leave, Bel went to *Uncle Gus's* Commissariat Specie Exchange to trade some of her credits for Llannonninn eents, bihts, luhmps and krelps.

There, she had what promised to be a most profitable conversation with Commissariat Faline Mahoud.

"Going down-planet?" Ven Mahoud spoke oh-so-casually. "Probably be the usual native artisans, pushing goods on you. Hand-made stuff, even stuff from local factories. Food. Liquor. That kind of thing."

"I wouldn't be surprised."

"It'd be nice to see some of that local stuff," Mahoud said. "It would take my mind off my troubles. For instance, the matter converter's been acting up. Program it for, say, a gross of boardwall pens, and it'll come out with something completely different. Like, maybe, those boots you put on your wish list but can't afford."

"The matter converter might accidentally produce just what I want in just my size?"

"Accidents do happen. If I didn't keep exact records, there's no telling what might come out of that machine."

"Yeah, you want to be careful."

"You be careful, too," Mahoud said. "If anybody saw you bringing down-planet goods in here, they might get the wrong idea when they saw you wearing those boots."

"I wouldn't dream of giving anybody the wrong idea," said Bel.

~*~

Lieutenant Commander Wotan Hessaphess, Duty Officer for the shore party, grinned with general-purpose malice and said, "Shore leave is restricted. The party is to descend into Jok'rel's Traveler's Rest Inn, stay there for twelve hours, and then return to the ship. Orders from the Captain, by request of the Grand Council of Llannonn."

There was some grumbling, though not from Bel. It's hard to grumble when your teeth are clenched.

"Ven Schuster, you don't seem to be a happy camper," said Hessaphess. "Do you have a complaint? Tell me all about it. That's what I'm here for."

Heavy sarcasm was Hessaphess's long suit.

"I thought shore leave meant getting away from it all," Bel said, sweet as pie. "Spending twelve hours in close quarters with the people you see every day of your life isn't getting away from it all, it's taking most of it with you."

The party members shot each other glum looks and edged apart.

"I'm not complaining," Bel said, mindful that a restricted leave beat no leave at all. "There won't be any Munchkins crawling under the tables looking to give somebody a laser hotfoot; that's one comfort. It's just not my idea of altogether satisfactory R & R."

"Think of it as a blessing in disguise," Hessaphess said,

with a smirk. "Not so much to confess."

Hessaphess, an engineer, hailed from the planet Indverdeen, which seemed to produce such a disproportionate number of engineers. He was also a specialist in the Relativity Bypass, Professor of Szoffomooric Physics, and a Scot by natural inclination. He had rigged a contraption to distill the sludge from the Relativity Bypass engines into a liquid with a radioactive half-life of ten minutes and which, when cool, could pass for 100-year-old Scotch. He was tight with a credit and, not being Catholic, he considered himself a Protestant.

He had the double helping of double-jointed elbows and knees which made tinkering through poorly-placed access panels more practicable for Inverdinians than for less articulated types. A brawny man, with raspberry skin, burgundy hair and cinnamon eyes, when in his cups he claimed to be built like a brick church door. He was certainly high and wide, and some carried the simile further by suggesting he was slightly unhinged.

"Nobody has to go who doesn't want to," Hessaphess said. "Anyone here want to decline leave?"

No one did.

The party consisted of instructors Bel Schuster and Tetra Petrie, Hessaphess, and eight civilian crew members. They huddled in the transfer dock, a large bare room with a glass-enclosed transfer module in one corner. Two technicians in the "mod box" waited for Hessaphess's order to effect transfer or, as the old science hands put it, to "punch a wormhole."

The physics of punching and riding wormholes from one place to another fills volumes. Once in place, though, the module could be worked with three simple controls: toggles marked OFF/ON and ACTIVATE, and a keypad marked COORDINATES with a plastic bubble taped over it to prevent idle fiddling. The ship's computer set the coordinates, using programmed information and Hobson's patented "common sense" circuits. It hardly ever messed up.

Hessaphess frowned at the technicians. "Coordinates set?"

One of the techs checked the monitor. "Set," she said.

"Activate."

The other technician flipped the switch.

And they were in the reception lounge the Inn had reserved for their arrival. It bore the unmistakable stamp of every Traveler's Rest Inn "just folks"-iness.

"Remember," Hessaphess said, "you can rent a room, you can swim, you can zero-gee, you can spend all twelve hours in the bar; but you can't, under any circumstances, leave the Inn. No exceptions, this means YOU. Understood?"

Everybody nodded. Everybody headed for the bar.

"Ven Hessaphess," said Bel, putting a hand on one of his right elbows.

"No exceptions," he repeated.

"No, of course not, certainly not, why, what a thought," said Bel. "I only wanted to ask if I could buy you a drink."

"Why?"

"What do you care?"

Wotan Hessaphess had never turned down a free drink in his life. He made his usual acceptance speech: "I'd love it, but I left my money belt in my other tunic."

"So, you can't buy a round in return. I understand. Don't think a thing of it. Listen, I've got specie burning a hole in my Capri pants and nothing much to spend it on. Let's have a bottle or two, my treat."

Hessaphess didn't mind if he did.

It didn't take Bel long to realize a barrel or two wouldn't have made any difference. The Inverdinian became elevated, yes, and told tall tales of engines he had known, alternating with spirited attempts at singing "A Mighty Fortress Is Our God," improvising where memory failed, but Hessaphess never forgot a direct order, and he never compromised.

Bel finally gave up. She bought him a final bottle and moved (somewhat unsteadily) to a dim and distant table, there to brood over the illustrated brochures from the rack in the lobby.

She wanted to see Llannonn. The more certain it appeared she wouldn't see it, at least on this leave, the more she wanted to. She wanted to wander, as free as one of the Wandering Tribes, collecting a judiciously selected bundle of easily portable souvenirs.

She wanted to see Council City's pastel soapstone towers and low-flying land-cars, maybe hire a pedicab powered by a handsome young man, and tour the city. She wanted to visit a Wandering Tribe's caravan and have her fortune told while the wild music of the scented twirlpipes made her senses reel. Or whatever.

But no. Here she sat and here she would stay, while the only locals who weren't giving the strangers the old fish-eye tried to sell them cheap bric-a-brac, or hustled games of chance.

Take, for instance, the woman sitting alone over there, in the double-breasted lilac jumpsuit with the plaid peplum. She was playing Solitary Coup d'Etat, in which one endeavored to overthrow one's own government — or, actually, to undermine one's own card tricks. One laid out two hands, and then things became increasingly complicated until one of the hands won. Or didn't.

This woman laid out the hands and played, but she did a poor job of losing, her mind obviously not on the game. She kept raking the room with furtive looks, winning trick after trick, and trying to pretend she didn't care. People didn't take the trouble to learn and play Coup d'Etat if they didn't care. Bel knew. She played.

Ah, well, if she had to be stuck here for twelve hours, she might as well spend some of them in congenial company. If the woman shared Bel's taste in cards, she might share her sense of humor. She might be a kindred spirit.

At any rate, she looked like she'd be easy to beat, even in Bel's current state of fading fuddle. If the woman could be persuaded to bet her earrings, or a handkerchief, or some other homely trinkets, the trip wouldn't be a total loss.

Or her jumpsuit. Ven Mahoud was too slender for it, but the woman and Bel shared the same build and coloring. *A new suit'll do me as well as a new pair of boots.*

Bel signaled to a waiter. "Say, Mack," she said, having reached the point of being pals with any old world you'd name.

"Yes, Galactic Union Tourist? How may I help you?"

"I'd like to buy the lady with the cards a drink," Bel said. "And ask her if she'd like to play me a round of Cut-throat, will you?"

The waiter bowed and left the table.

Meanwhile, the woman had fastened her attention on Bel, who gestured to herself and to the cards. The woman nodded, shuffled, and laid out a game of double-handed Coup as Bel joined her.

At two other dim and distant tables, two shadowy figures noted the move.

One, a male Stokk, saw it with complacence. It seemed to answer a question for him in a way he found reassuring. He kept the table under watch, but only just.

The other, an Earthling male, was riveted. He had sunk behind the fernlike foliage of a potted plant when Wotan Hessaphess — or, rather, when Wotan Hessaphess's Trooper uniform — entered. Now, he almost slipped into what light the bar could boast in the intensity of his interest.

"Ah," he said, with a wolfish grin and a twirl of his mustache points. "I see. Yes, I see."

Chapter 4

Earlier that day.

Freldt Saymak looked warily around the all-but-empty barroom of Jok'rel's Traveler's Rest Inn and laid out another game of Solitary Coup d'Etat. She wondered if she was doing the smart thing. Oh, it was the *right* thing, no question, but smart and right aren't always the same, especially when criminal activity is involved.

Freldt discarded a high card and drew what she hoped was a lower one. It wasn't.

How long would she have to wait? So far, Innkeeper Knosh Jok'rel hadn't questioned his bookkeeper's hanging around the bar on her day off. *Probably glad of the money.*

So here Freldt was, waiting, hours early, but unable to sit at home and watch the time pass. *And what about District Criminal Investigator Pel Darzin or his operative?* Was one of them here, even now? Was the shadowy figure at that dim and distant table one of them? Was *that* one?

The lobby door swung open and a stream of people entered. One of them, a large, broad, red man with any number of joints, wore the uniform of a Galactic Union Space Trooper.

He and a woman in black Capri pants and a flowered jersey sat at a table near the drink dispenser and called for a bottle of the best.

Freldt continued to dart searching glances around the room. This, and the noise the Trooper made, howling or singing or something, distracted her from her game. Any other time, she would've been irritated, would've sent a sharply worded note to the Trooper on the back of her personal card, but today she couldn't concentrate enough to notice how badly she played.

The woman in the pretty shirt moved to a nearby table and began looking through travel brochures.

Odd. The staff of Jok'rel's had been told the tourists were confined to the Inn. So why would one of them be looking at travel brochures?

Of course. How clever. District Criminal Investigator Pel Darzin must have realized the Stokk Gord Pron might be here ahead of time, and had sent in his operative disguised as an off-world tourist. The constabulary was probably working some cases in concert with the Space Troopers, now that Llannonn might join the Galactic Union.

Freldt saw the operative signal to a waiter, heard the operative mutter, "Saymak," and saw her table indicated. She watched the waiter bow and move off.

The operative made a series of furtive gestures, suggesting they pretend to have a chance meeting over cards.

Freldt nodded, shuffled, and laid out the cards for a game of double-handed Coup as the operative joined her.

"I am Bookkeeper Freldt Saymak," Freldt said, feeling rather foolish, telling the operative something she obviously knew. Still, the courtesies should be observed. It cost nothing, and it kept things clear and pleasant.

"And I am, uh," the operative hesitated over the lie, "Galactic Union Tourist Bel Schuster."

Chapter 5

Bel introduced herself to the card-player, remembering, just in time, to give a herself a descriptive title.

Bookkeeper Freldt Saymak seemed less antsy as she dealt cards for two. Bel wondered if she supplemented her bookkeeper's income with card sharping; maybe she thought she'd hooked a sucker. Maybe she was just lonely.

Her next words echoed Bel's thoughts.

"I'm so glad you've come. I haven't seen anyone I know come in."

"The day is young," Bel said.

Freldt lost the last of her jitters in the face of this professional placidity. "Your work must require a lot of patience," she said.

Now, how does she know I'm a teacher? Does it show? "A *lot* of patience," Bel said. "And how."

They played three games, each time reducing one another's hands to chaotic jumbles. Both took satisfaction in this outcome, the object of Coup d'Etat being to make the other guy lose, rather than to win, oneself.

And all the time, Bel had her eye on Freldt's jumpsuit, peplum and earrings. Finally, she said, "Nice outfit."

"Thank you. I've been admiring yours."

"Have you, now? Well." Bel gathered the cards into a stack and shuffled. "What do you say to a trade?"

"A trade?"

"Your suit for mine. We've got the same build, about the same height, look to be about the same heft. We could go to the ladies' room and switch. Both get a new outfit out of it."

Freldt understood. *What a relief! Dear, clever operative!* They would trade clothes, and the operative would take her place. The Stokk Gord Pron would spew his nasty criminal innuendos directly to an officer of the law, and she, Bookkeeper Freldt Saymak, would be out of the loop.

"Yes! Wonderful idea!"

She led the way back through the lobby and into a room with "Female Humanoid" stenciled on the door in Llannonninn and Allesesperanto.

They changed and stood side-by-side before the wall-sized screen (so much more realistic than a mirror, as it showed you what you really looked like, rather than what you would look like if you were put together backward).

"I was right," Bel said. "They fit fine. They look good on us, too, don't you think so?" Lilac had always been Bel's color.

To Freldt, how well they looked didn't matter. What mattered to her was that the operative had the same hair, skin, and eye color as she did, or close enough to pass to the unsubtle eyes of a Stokk.

"Should we both go back to the table?" Freldt adjusted the collar of her new blouse. "Or should I leave now?"

Leave? While you still have your jewelry? "Oh, stay," said Bel. "Maybe I can get those earrings off of you."

"My earrings! Of course!" Freldt blushed. Lucky Operative Bel Schuster was so good at her job. She removed the baubles and gave them to Bel, who put them on.

"Stick around for a while," Bel said. *I think I've got a live one.*

As they passed through the lobby, a beefy man hunched himself over the brochure rack and watched them out of the corners of his eyes.

Another operative, thought Freldt.

Weirdo, thought Bel.

They went back to the table. It amused Bel when Freldt

Saymak took the seat Bel had had before, leaving her to take Freldt's. Obviously, the woman did have a sense of humor.

They were no sooner seated, when the man from the lobby slipped into the bar and oozed around to a dim and distant table behind a potted plant.

Freldt congratulated herself: *I spotted him as an operative when I first saw him, before Operative Bel Schuster ever came in.* She wanted to point the man out to Operative Bel Schuster, to make up for her slip with the earrings, but she refrained.

Wotan Hessaphess wobbled over and clapped Freldt on the shoulder.

He saluted the empty bottle at his table. "How about anooder? Anurder? Another?"

Freldt looked to Bel for help. Bel nodded, and Freldt said, "Fine."

"Fine," Hessaphess said. "Call out the reserves, eh? Where's the little Trooper's room?"

Freldt gave him directions, and he maneuvered himself away.

"Isn't he on duty?" Freldt watched him weave his way out. "Should he be drinking?"

"He might walk funny," Bel said sourly, "and he might talk funny, but nothing could make him think funny. What I don't get is, why did he mooch a bottle off you? He'll take anything he's offered, but I've never known him to panhandle before."

Freldt laughed. "Don't you see? We fooled even him."

Fooled him? He thought she was me? She stared hard at the Llannonninn woman. *We do look a lot alike. Yes, we do.*

This opened up a panorama of opportunity. Not that Bel would ever take advantage of such opportunity by going off-limits. At least, not very far off-limits.

But what would it hurt to go outside the Inn? Just outside. Just step out, and get a lungful of alien air. What harm could it do? She hadn't asked Wotan Hessaphess if she could at least do that much; if she had asked him, he probably would've said yes. Certainly, he would have. Why, it was almost as if she *had* asked him, and he had given her permission.

"One more hand," Bel said, and dealt the cards.

When Wotan Hessaphess returned to his table, there were half a dozen bottles upon it. "Compliments of the lady," the waiter said.

Hessaphess waved happily and uncorked the first.

Bel lost the hand. A bit of a waste; she was so intent on her new plan, she didn't have a bet on the game.

Bel worked the tension out of her shoulders, yawned, and said, "Think I'll get up and stretch my legs. Will you excuse me?"

"Yes, of course," said Freldt. She felt as if a poisoned cup had passed from her. Her part in all this was over. The switch had been made, and had worked. Now the operative would meet or draw off the Stokk Gord Pron, and Freldt could relax. She ordered herself a drink and laid the cards aside.

She watched Operative Bel Schuster leave the room. Sure enough, the Stokk Gord Pron detached himself from the shadows of one of the dim and distant tables and followed her. It made Freldt shiver to think he had been there all the time, and what it would have meant if Operative Bel Schuster's ploy hadn't worked.

The other operative, the beefy man from the lobby, pushed the ferns out of his face and followed, too.

Freldt watched in approval. *Very efficient. There go a couple of people who know what they're doing.*

~*~

Bel, meanwhile, crossed the lobby to the Inn's front entrance.

She heard the barroom door open and checked to make sure Wotan Hessaphess wasn't following her. No, only a Stokk, a slick-looking, snappy dresser with Kelly green hair and lemon yellow skin. She smiled at him, and he smiled back, his lipless mouth showing his good teeth to advantage.

Bel went into the vestibule. From here, she could look through the Inn's glass front into the street.

The Stokk came into the vestibule, too.

He seemed about to speak to her. Bel didn't want him to speak to her — him, or anyone else. She wanted to be left alone, to look and enjoy.

She frowned and shook her head, and went out.

Out, into the street, where she had no business being.

Bel took a deep breath of the unfamiliar air. It had a different taste than Earth or shipboard air, different smells; it even seemed to have a different texture.

She could go to the corner without violating directives *too* much. She could go to the corner and stand there, people-watch for a few minutes, then go back, and none the wiser.

A food vendor on the corner offered a soup made of fish and wine, and edible tiles made of dried meat spread with herbed cheese.

Bel bought and ate some, washing it down with carbonated fruit juice bought from another vendor on the far corner. Still on the same block as the hotel, you see, just outside the walls; a mere eight inches or so from where she ought to be; practically still inside.

Someone touched her on the arm. She turned, half-expecting the Stokk, but finding, instead, a bag lady.

The lady's thick black hair was streaked with white and twisted into nets on either side of her head. She wore an ankle-length dress covered with so many flounces and ribbons Bel couldn't guess at her figure, and she carried so many bags so full of so much stuff it was a wonder she could walk.

She put her bags down to clutch Bel's arm.

"You're being followed, dear," she whispered. "Why are you being followed? Have you done something you shouldn't have? Do you want to tell me about it?"

"No," said Bel. "Thank you. I'm all right."

"Shall I call someone for you? Do you need help?"

"No," said Bel again. "Thank you. I'm fine."

She shouldn't have smiled at that Stokk. He probably thought she'd been flirting with him. *Ick.* Maybe she'd better get back.

From the next corner came a whistle and a hum, and a burst of heavy perfume. *Scented twirlpipes?*

Well, she could get back by finishing the square as well as by retracing her steps.

Bel put a hand in her pocket. She wasn't exactly rolling in credits. Still, it seemed greedy to keep it for herself when this poor old kind-of-crazy bag lady stood at her elbow. "Do you need any money?"

"For what?"

Bel smiled in what she hoped was an unprovoking way and went to find the twirlpipes.

Chapter 6

Rewind. Change angle. Replay scene.

At a corner table of the nearly empty barroom, where almost none of the faint light could penetrate, sat a Stokk. To give him his planet's courtesy title, there sat Gunjin Gord Pron.

Gord Pron was quite a lady's man on Stokk. His eyebrows and shoulder-length layered hair were a bright yellowish-green. This, coupled with his clear yellow skin, made him the Stokk equivalent of "tall, dark, and handsome." His beady black eyes focused on Freldt Saymak.

He had anticipated she might arrive early, perhaps to meet someone. Say, the District Criminal Investigator, just for an example. So Gunjin Pron had been outside earlier, watching from the service alley.

He usually didn't mind lurking in alleys: He wouldn't like it known, but he had a secret soft spot for alley jammers, with their prehensile toes and their wrinkly pink noses. Today, though, he couldn't let himself be distracted. Today, he had to forgo the challenge of spotting the color-altering vermin against their various backgrounds. Today, he had to deny himself the pleasure of playing with the adorable bundles of fluff by chucking bits of concrete at their dear little heads.

When he had seen Freldt arrive, he had slipped in at the back while she went through the lobby.

He decided he would keep watch for another hour or so, until slightly past the time agreed. He wanted to make sure. That's how you stayed free, safe, and alive: You made sure.

Pron hoped Saymak hadn't called the constabulary. Roughing people up was part of Stokk culture, but sometimes what started out as a spot of casual, social brutality slipped into a habit, and then into an addiction. Pron had caught himself in time, but he knew how slight a nudge it would take to push him over the edge.

Gunjin Boktu Jippir wouldn't like it if he went over the edge. Gunjin Jippir was a man of refinement. He liked his harassments incremental and his punishments finely adjusted. A berserker had no honor in Gunjin Jippir's estimation. Gunjin Jippir was an uptown kind of guy, and a berserker was strictly for the sticks.

Gunjin Pron licked the rim of his mouth. Saymak hadn't called the constabulary. He wouldn't let himself even think it. She would sit there, waiting for him, until he joined her at her table and she told him she'd do what he wanted. Then he'd go back to Boktu Jippir and report success.

And if she refused? Pron clenched his fists so tightly they paled to flax, and the fine hairs on his knuckles stood out like grass.

Calmly, now. He'd talk to her again, that's what he'd do. Explain things to her again, break a finger, and give her another chance.

Pron was nothing, if not a gentleman.

At another corner table, near a potted fern, sat an Earthling, and oh, but he was a naughty boy. From the coarse, tight waves of his pepper-and-salt hair to the square-toed boots on his oversized feet, every beefy, big-boned inch of him proclaimed the rascal. His eyes were a heavenly blue, and his pepper-and-salt mustache was waxed and twirled to the primmest of points. But those eyes held twinkles far from heavenly, and there was something about that mustache, something rakish in the twirl, or in the wide white smile so often spread beneath it, or in the cavernous dimples it spanned like a pair of railroad bridges.

There was no smile now, nor any dimples.

Force of Habit

Connell Morgan had been drawn to Llannonn by rumors of the congenital gullibility of its natives. Though undeniably true, the rumors failed to mention the natives' innate quickness at wising up to any particular scam. Some kind of defense mechanism, Morgan supposed.

It wasn't possible for Morgan to run out of scams, but coming up with new ones in such rapid order felt uncomfortably like work. Even worse, his credibility was beginning to slip.

So far, he had kept clear of the law by charming his pigeons before plucking them; so far, they had always been willing to forgive and forget. But word spread, and it was only a matter of time before the government made a case against him in its own name and brought in witnesses, willing or no. They would have to hire a bus. Two.

Morgan had come to the Inn's barroom this afternoon to monitor the atmospheric conditions, as it were. He had been working the room for several evenings, now. He thought the time had probably come to move on, but hated to leave a hunting ground while the game still ran thick.

So, he came in early, to read the attitudes of the bartender and the waiters, to gauge the reactions of his victims as they drifted in and saw him at his usual table. If nobody warned him off, with words or with "just you wait" expressions, he'd do as much business as he could tonight and skip town.

Rather skip planet. Shooting fish in a barrel is an easy way to get a meal, but it doesn't exactly hone your skills.

So far, everything tested normal.

Then the door opened, and horror walked into the barroom.

The horror was preceded by four men, four women, and a child. No, four men and five women, one of them very small. Horror was accompanied by a woman in black Capri pants and a flowered jersey. Horror covered the exterior of an Inverdinian with the look of a terrible thirst upon him.

It was the uniform of the Galactic Union Space Troopers.

Connell Morgan shrank back into the shadows. With the toe of one of his boots, he hooked the fern's pot and slid it into a more concealing position.

~*~

The advent of the Galactic Unionites irritated the Stokk momentarily. They had nothing to do with his goals; they were clutter. Still, Saymak continued to sit alone, and looked to Pron as if she would be alone until he moved to keep her company.

Pron glanced at the timepiece on the wall of the bar. Another half-hour, and he'd go over.

In the meantime, he amused himself by trying to tell the newcomers apart. When he singled one out, he gave it a name. He called the red one with the extra joints and the Trooper uniform "Blaze." Then, there was the short one; Pron called her "Bitesize." The female sitting with Blaze, Pron called "Flower," because he could only tell her from the others by her flowered top.

Flower moved to a table by herself, probably frightened by the roars of her companion. Pron had just noted he hadn't long to wait, when Flower moved again. To Freldt's table.

Pron relaxed, watching Freldt deal Flower some cards. Freldt couldn't have been hoping to meet an officer, then, or she would have told the stranger to buzz off, which she undoubtedly would as soon after fourteen hundred hours as possible.

Freldt looked calm, which she surely wouldn't if she planned to make any trouble for herself. He might not have to break a finger, after all. Well, he could always hope.

~*~

Connell Morgan kept an eye on the Trooper. He didn't appear to be looking for anybody. He didn't appear to be circulating a description. What he appeared to be doing was getting a good hearty snootful of hard liquor.

The Trooper wasn't buying. The woman in the flowered top was buying, and she was buying big.

Then the woman moved to another table and began looking through travel brochures.

Morgan's waiter came by to see if he wanted anything.

He wanted information, information being part of his stock in trade. "Who are those people?"

"Tourists," the waiter said. "Shore leave, actually, from a teaching ship or something."

"Sightseers?"

The waiter shook his head. "Confined to the premises." He darted a pained glance at the Trooper. "I can see why."

Morgan took another beer and paid his tab. *So why is the big spender looking at travel brochures?*

Even as he asked himself the question, the big spender moved to yet another table, where she fell into violent cardplay and guarded conversation with another woman, one who had been there all along, probably a native.

Connell looked from one woman to the other, then to the Trooper, who had just noticed he was sitting alone and talking to himself.

"Ah," he said, and twirled his mustache. "I see. Yes, I see."

~*~

Gord Pron thought nothing of it when Freldt Saymak and Flower stood and left the barroom. Being a lady's man, he was well-acquainted with the genetically programmed desire of women for company when moving through public rooms. They would be back soon.

~*~

Connell Morgan slipped, as inconspicuously as possible, into the lobby after the women. He was in time to see them go into the Female Humanoids' room.

The longer he waited, the more certain he felt that he had read the situation right. When they came back through the lobby wearing one another's clothing, he knew.

He counted to five and followed them back into the bar. It wouldn't do to lose track of his quarry now.

They had switched places, as well as clothes.

The Trooper dredged himself up from his seat and went over to them. He spoke to the wrong one, and neither of the women corrected his mistake. The Trooper left the barroom, came back, and reseated himself, keeping their table in sight.

Morgan held his breath as the woman who'd come in with the Trooper yawned and left, this time, alone.

The Trooper didn't move, except to toss a playful cork at the table of tourists who'd come in with him.

Morgan waited until some Stokk guy cleared the door, then pushed aside the ferns and followed his prey.

~*~

Gord Pron saw Freldt and Flower return, just as he'd known they would. Blaze came over and talked to Flower, left the barroom, and returned.

Then, the unexpected. Freldt got up and walked out.

What was wrong with the woman? Was she insane, to leave before he'd shown up?

Then he realized what must have happened. She had seen him here, after all. She had assumed he meant to wait for her cardmate to leave. She had tried to ditch her outside, but had failed. So she was ditching her now, trusting him to understand and follow her into the lobby.

He did so.

Saymak smiled when she saw him. He smiled back. Yes, he'd read the signs aright.

She went into the vestibule, a strange choice of meeting places. He didn't like it. The vestibule would be open to any eyes on one side, and shielded for listening ears on the other. Yet, he followed.

He drew breath to tell her she'd have to do better than this, but she frowned at him.

Frowned, and shook her head, and took to the safety of the

open street.

Fool! She didn't think it would be so easy, did she? All streets weren't crowded, and when she reached one that wasn't, she'd find him there. Sooner or later, he'd catch her alone, and then he'd teach her to brush him off with a come-on and a frown.

~*~

Connell Morgan loafed along behind his target. That fool Stokk was loitering, getting in the way. Morgan wished somebody would come and arrest the Stokk for creating a nuisance.

~*~

Nearly time. District Criminal Investigator Pel Darzin looked through the Traveler's Inn's vestibule's glass and stepped swiftly back.

A woman in a double-breasted lilac jumpsuit with a plaid peplum stood looking out.

The Stokk Gord Pron entered the vestibule. The woman frowned, shook her head at him, and left the building. Pron came out, too.

Surely, this was Bookkeeper Freldt Saymak. Right color skin, right color hair, right outfit.

But what had happened? Had she expected him to come early, and come early herself? Had the Stokk done the same thing? Had they spoken? Argued? Was she looking for an officer now?

Apparently, she was looking for lunch. In fact, once she left the Inn, Bookkeeper Freldt Saymak seemed to become unaware of the Stokk's existence.

She meandered down the street, the Stokk nearly at her heels, District Criminal Investigator Pel Darzin a discreet distance behind.

~*~

Connell Morgan trailed the big spender and awaited his chance.

Chapter 7

Meanwhile, back aboard the *Uncle Gus*, Captain Joan A. "Jinx" Fazzaria stepped into a transfer alcove near her quarters and punched the locus code for the bridge.

Captain Joan A. Fazzaria, an American Earthling, had skin the color of a roasted coffee bean and eyes the color of caramel. She wore her black hair in one long braid brought up onto the crown of her head and doubled under, forming a sort of crest. 5'11" to begin with, this crest, and the low heels of her boots, made her top six feet.

She would've been imposing, but her cheeks were so rosy, her voice so soft, and her fingernails so badly bitten, no one could fear her wrath. Much.

An electronic voice strung together prerecorded phrases to say, "You have selected locus . . . A1, the bridge. There are . . . three . . . terminals at that location. Terminal one is . . . temporarily out of service. Terminal two is . . . currently in use. Terminal three is . . . temporarily out of service. Press 1, if you wish to select an alternate locus; 2, if you wish to enter transfer queue; 3, to report a malfunction."

Captain Fazzaria pressed 2 and hoped terminal two would stay in service long enough to get her to her post. She did not sigh. She did not look deep within herself for one last shred of patience. She was Jinx Fazzaria, and this was the *Uncle Gus*, and she was used to it.

Troopers knew that luck was real. There were lucky ships, lucky Captains, lucky troopers. Jinx was a lucky Captain, but Jinx's luck was bad. Jinx had gremlins in her pockets; hence, her nickname. The Powers That Be tried to maintain the fiction that the Troopers didn't really hold with silly folklore stuff, but they still transferred Jinx out of active service. To the *St. Gregory the Wonderworker*, AKA *Uncle Gus*.

"A terminal at locus . . . A1, the bridge, is . . . now available. Press 1, if you wish to transfer to this locus; 2, if you—"

Jinx pressed 1 and stepped onto the bridge.

"Somebody call Maintenance," she said. "Terminals one and three up here are. . . ." She trailed off, seeing Maintenance already at work.

"All systems fully functional, Ven Chestney?"

"Practically, Captain."

"Specify, Ven Chestney. Specify." Captain Fazzaria sat in the command chair at the rear of the bridge. More of a post or a console than a chair, it had banks of displays and monitors on either side and keypads accessing the ship's computer on either arm. Lieutenant Commander Harold Chestney, *Uncle Gus's* First Mate, sat at a console of his own, nearby. He was a Muscular Christian, and an All-American Hero, and had this tendency to want to solve disagreements by wrestling people to the ground and reasoning with them.

"Navigation is still running the trouble-shooting program. Should finish in, I don't know, real soon now."

Harry Chestney had been surplussed, too; oh, yes, Harry had been surplussed.

All the Troopers aboard the *Uncle Gus* had been surplussed. Jinx knew it, and it did nothing for her self-esteem, or for her peace of mind, either. Nor did the ship's name: St. Gregory the Wonderworker was one of the patron saints of lost causes and desperate situations. So the ship's chaplain, Brother Theodore, said, anyway, and he should know. Jinx was a Baptist, herself.

"All systems go, Captain," said Chestney. "Check and double-check." He handed her a display screen the size and thickness of a clipboard.

Jinx checked it again, okayed it with her thumbprint, and returned it to Chestney. Bridge business over, she relaxed formality. "Thank you, Harry," she said. "How long before we break orbit?"

"Nine hours, thirty-six minutes."

As Chestney spoke, Ven Meichi, the civilian Communications Specialist, also an Earthling, began pressing finger pads on her console.

"Captain!"

"Yes, Donna, what is it?"

"A call from Llannonn, Captain. From the Grand Council Chamber in Council City."

Jinx and Chestney exchanged wary looks.

"Specify caller," the Captain said.

Donna Meichi pressed some more pads, and said, "Councilor Thomms Nyakk, of the Urbanites."

"I'll take it here," the Captain said. She swung a visiscreen up and over from the side of the command chair and clicked it on. "Monitor and record."

"Yes, Captain."

A man appeared on the Captain's screen.

"Captain Joan A. Fazzaria?"

"Yes."

"I am Councilor Thomms Nyakk."

"Yes," said the Captain. "Of the Urbanites, I'm told."

"You're well-informed, Captain."

"Thank you. Councilor, please be aware our conversation is being monitored and recorded by a crewmember and the ship's computer, and will be filed with the daily communications log for review by the Space Troopers Contact Board. Is this understood?"

"Yes."

"Is this acceptable?"

"Yes. And you please be aware no one, I hope, is monitoring or recording this call on our end."

Uh-oh. "How may we help you, Councilor?"

"I'm sure you know the General Council are debating the question of joining the Galactic Union," Nyakk said.

"Yes."

"Some of us are passionately in favor of the move, others are just as passionately against it. My own party is split. In fact, Councilor Bella Yozgat, my fellow Urbanite on the Grand Council, is one of the most violently opposed. She heads the Llannonn for the Llannonninn movement."

He seemed to expect some input, so Jinx said, "Please continue."

"Councilor Bella Yozgat's always trying to whip up anti-Galactic Union feelings in the General Council. Lately, she seems to be making some progress."

"I'm sorry to hear that," Jinx said, wondering if he expected her to do something about it.

"There's a criminal loose in Council City," Nyakk went on. "A male Galactic Unionite, apparently an Earthling. We're only starting to get complaints against him, but he's been fouling the city for months, and his crimes are like nothing we've ever seen before."

Jinx crossed her fingers and hoped the Councilor wouldn't give her any details. Jinx had a weak stomach.

For once, a better kind of luck was with her, because Nyakk moved closer to his point.

"Councilor Bella Yozgat is using this criminal as an example of what we can expect from closer contact with off-worlders. Of course, we have other off-worlders on Llannonn than Galactic Unionites. The Stokk are nothing to write home about, if you ask me. But she's using all her venom on the Union."

Doesn't sound good. Doesn't sound good. Could I put in for retirement? Now?

"Captain Joan A. Fazzaria," said the Councilor, "it was Councilor Bella Yozgat who had your shore party restricted to Jok'rel's Traveler's Rest Inn."

"Oh?"

"The criminal I just told you about has been frequenting Jok'rel's," Nyakk said, his eyes more red than brown with the force of his emphasis. "Our District Criminal Investigator and his officers will be there this evening to make an arrest."

"Oh," said Jinx.

"Do you want your people there, when the arrest is made? Do you want the Galactic Union and the Space Troopers associated with that arrest, with that criminal, in the slightest degree? Do you want all the papers to run pictures of the criminal against a backdrop of your shore party?"

"No," said Jinx. "No. No, I don't. I most definitely do not. No."

"Then I'd advise you to recall them immediately. When the arrest has been made, I'll see the papers specifically mention the absence of any Galactic Unionites, other than the criminal himself, at the scene. Your shore party can come back, then, probably without restriction."

"We appreciate your help, Councilor," said Jinx. "And in return?"

"In return what?"

"Exactly."

"Exactly what?"

"In return, exactly, what? You've done the Union a service, possibly an important service. What should the Union do for you, in return?"

"Oh." Nyakk appeared to be giving the matter some thought. "Say 'thank you'?"

"Thank you?"

"Thank *you*, Captain Joan A. Fazzaria," said the Councilor, stroking his pockmarked cheek. "Thank *you*. From a great many of us with longer memories than my 'esteemed colleague' can boast." Jinx had forgotten the koepox epidemic afflicting Llannonn at the time the Galactic Union had made first contact, and the mercy run which had brought serum to the planet. Apparently, others had also forgotten. Fortunately, Thomms Nyakk hadn't.

The Councilor broke contact, and Jinx swung her screen back down against her chair.

Jinx addressed her First Mate. "You heard?"

Chestney nodded.

Jinx raised her right hand to her mouth and bit a nail. "Should we do it?"

"Recall the shore party? Or send them back, when the smoke clears?"

"Either one. Both."

"What do *you* think?" Harry hadn't gotten to be a Lieutenant Commander by sticking his neck out when he should have been covering the opposite point of the compass.

"I think we should definitely recall the shore party. As for sending them back, I don't know. I could PHAX Sector Command."

"Shall I FAR an RFD?"

"Yes. Yes, do. And send a copy of the call along with it."

"Yes, Captain."

Chestney went to his console.

"Ven Meichi."

"Yes, Captain?"

"Call Lieutenant Commander Hessaphess and order him to have the shore party back in the reception lounge at 1215 hours. Tell him to signal when ready to board."

"Yes, Captain."

"Then call the transfer dock and tell them to prepare to pipe the shore party aboard at 1215 hours. Tell them to wait for Hessaphess's signal."

"Yes, Captain."

Maybe my luck is changing. After all, here's a crisis averted, or at least a black eye to the Union deflected. This might put her in pretty good with the brass hats at Sector Command. Word might even rise higher. Maybe she'd get transferred off this flying fruitcake before she went gently and completely loony.

Take, for instance, the deal (if you could call it a deal) she'd just cut with Councilor Thomms Nyakk. He gives her a juicy piece of intelligence, then expects her to believe he isn't going to call in the IOU sometime. And she believed him.

That frightened her.

Still, the shore party was being recalled, and the Union's fat would be out of the soup when the fire hit the fan. Or something like that.

Jinx sincerely hoped she had made the right decision. She did *not* want to end her military career pushing a broom around the corroding carcasses in Podunk Drydock.

"Time, Ven Chestney?"

"1215, Captain."

"Hessaphess should be signaling any minute now."

"Yes, Captain."

He wouldn't do it. He would misunderstand the order. Or he'd get the time wrong. Or his squawkbox wouldn't work. Or the transfer module would be on the blink. Something.

"I have Hessaphess's signal," said Donna Meichi.

It would be the module, then. Jinx's finger rested on the keypad to raise Maintenance.

"And transfer dock has piped them aboard."

Jinx's finger twitched. "Repeat?"

"Ven Hessaphess and the shore party are aboard, Captain."

Jinx moved her hand from the keypad and pretended she had never had any doubt. "Thank you, Donna."

The party was back, safely, intact and without a hitch. *Miracles never cease.*

Chapter 8

Bel meant to follow the twirlpiper only as far as the corner. As soon as he reached the corner, she meant to turn away and finish her circuit of the block; to get back to the barroom before she got. . . . Before she caused. . . . Before much more time had passed.

But the piper played a merry tune, and the spicy floral scent was irresistible. Another block or two wouldn't be too far away, she reasoned. If she kept the Inn in sight, she could hurry right back as soon as the piper paused for breath.

She would have done it, too. She really would have. But. Bel wasn't the only tourist in town. A crowd collected around the twirlpiper; trailed him, as Bel trailed him. And where there's a crowd, there's a criminal.

"What th— Hey! Cut it out!" Bel found herself struggling with a hand for possession of her money belt.

The hand won.

"Hey!"

People shouted after the thief. They grabbed for the elusive hand and its owner but only grasped one another. The hand — and the money belt — vanished into the city.

"Perhaps I can be of service," said a man's voice.

Bel looked around and up. The man was over six feet tall, beefy, bluff, and hearty, with pepper-and-salt hair and a mustache twirled into points.

He said, "We were fellow patrons at the Inn just now. Perhaps you saw me there."

Oh, yes, the weirdo who'd been eying her from the brochure rack in the lobby.

"I see you did," he said. "I'm afraid I stared, didn't I? A weakness of mine, staring at beauty."

"Uh-huh." *Could that possibly have been any smarmier? No. No, it couldn't.*

"I saw that shocking daylight robbery," said the man. "You must report it to the officers." His smooth, mellifluous, baritone voice held just a touch of an Irish lilt.

"Well, but I have to get back." Bel hated to see a roll of hard-earned credits fade into the middle distance, but there's only so far you can stretch a tether. She judged she'd about reached this one's limit.

"You don't understand," the man said. "You *must* report it to the officers. It's the law."

"I'll tell them at the Inn." *Oh, yeah?* And let it be known she'd been out on the town?

"Reports of criminal victimization must be made in person, I'm afraid."

Not good. "I don't think—"

"Silly, isn't it, when it's just a formality? They don't even ask your name and address."

Maybe not so bad.

"Still, the law's the law, and the law must have its way, mustn't it?" The man smiled broadly. He had big, blocky teeth; the teeth of a bone-cruncher.

"I suppose it must," said Bel. Who knew what might happen if she didn't make this report? She didn't know much about Llannonn, after all; failing to report a crime might be a Federal case. This guy might be a government spy or something. He might blow the whistle on her if she tried to duck out.

"It won't take a minute," the man said. "The station house is just up the street."

"How far up the street?" She could see a few more sights. Maybe she could pick up a pen or a matchbook or something at the station house.

"Please, let me escort you. No chance of your getting lost,

you see. Then I'll bring you right back here. How does that sound?"

"It sounds like a lot of trouble for you. If it's just up the street, I can find my way back. But thanks for the offer."

"Not at all. It's part of my job."

The man took Bel's elbow and steered her around the piper and his fans.

"It is? What *is* your job?"

"Tourist Assistance," the man said, turning the full power of his innocent blue eyes on Bel.

This guy is full of it. Not that she felt a premonition of what was coming. Not a twinge. It was just a general observation. But she went along. That smashing smile; those blue, blue eyes.

"Just up here." He put his hand on her waist, guiding her into an alley.

Bel slammed on the brakes. "Where? This is an alley, Bub. I don't see any—"

He dropped behind Bel and threw an arm around her neck. "Come along quietly, and you won't get hurt," he said.

This move works better if you aren't twice as broad as your target. As it was, Bel's elbow caught him square in the sternum.

He let her go and put his hands to his chest. Bel picked up a piece of nameless but hefty debris and swung it. He deflected the blow with his arm and grabbed for her again.

A chittering and skittering suggested consternation among the alley's native wildlife. Jammy pandas, or something, Bel vaguely recalled, in that quiet part of her brain that was trying to pretend this wasn't happening.

She jumped out of his reach and looked around. She spotted a wall at the far end of the alley. There might be a cross-street there, or it might be a dead end; she couldn't tell. Better to stay as close as possible to this end of the alley, and try to get past Blue-eyes, here.

"There's no way out," the man said, one hand still held to the center of his chest. His voice remained smooth, though it had an understandable edge to it. "I'm not going to hurt you, you know. Just come with me."

"I fancy I see myself," said Bel, meaning *No.*

She feinted to one side, then rushed at the other.

He shifted toward her feint, and back toward her rush. He kept to the middle of the way, too close for her to chance passing him on either side, and Bel had to back up again.

Footsteps sounded beyond the man, at the mouth of the alley.

"Oh, dear," said a voice dripping with sarcasm, "I do hope I'm not interrupting something."

The beefy man glanced back over his shoulder. Bel took advantage, and swung her piece of debris. The man grabbed it, and tried to twist it away.

Bel hung on. Her feet left the ground. Her head hit a wall, and she knew no more.

~*~

Gunjin Gord Pron followed Bel, believing he followed Freldt, closely as she left the Inn. He hoped the threat of his near presence would make some impression on her, but she pretended she didn't notice him. She bought some food and a beverage.

Then a Wandering Tribeswoman dropped her bags and clutched the bookkeeper's arm. She spoke urgently to her for several minutes.

Freldt shook her head at the woman and moved on.

Now Pron understood. The officers, a nosy bunch of busybodies, had sniffed out their meeting, somehow, and had them under watch. Freldt had slipped away from them, smiling when she saw him follow her, warning him with a frown and a head shake. Now she pretended to wander aimlessly, looking for a chance to give him her real answer.

Clever! Pron began considering ways to try to cheat on

his side of the deal with Freldt, his people's form of showing admiration for another's guile.

Pron dropped back, to give Freldt more room to maneuver.

—*Now what?* There was some disturbance in the crowd Freldt had joined. A child broke from the mob and disappeared down a maze of service ways.

Now Freldt and a man left the crowd and moved ahead of it. It must be someone she knew; this was hardly the time to make a pickup. Or another officer in disguise?

Pron followed.

Freldt and her man turned into an alley. Pron turned in, too, to see the man blocking the way, and Freldt feinting at him with some kind of club.

A fine time to engage in romantic horseplay!

"Oh, dear," he said, "I do hope I'm not interrupting something."

The man glanced over his shoulder at the Stokk. Freldt took advantage — *What a woman!* — and tried to clip him with her club.

The man was worthy of her, though. He slung her up against the wall, knocking her out and getting her weapon all in one move.

"This is none of your business," the man growled, shaking the club at Pron.

Pron spread his lipless mouth in a smile and his open hands in concession.

After all, what could be better? The man would carry his love off to his arena, and any officers who might still be trying to keep an eye on her would go home.

Freldt and her man were obviously well-matched; they would occupy one another's interest for some time after she regained consciousness. So now, Pron would follow Freldt's sweetheart to his arena, then go report to Gunjin Boktu Jippir and receive new orders.

Pron let the man turn down the cross-street at the far end of the alley and darted softly after him.

~*~

District Criminal Investigator Pel Darzin had a time keeping an eye on the Stokk Gord Pron, let alone Bookkeeper Freldt Saymak. Pron moved forward, dropped back, sidled around corners.

Then Pron took off, hot-footing it around a twirlpiper and the crowd they always gathered, and down the street beyond.

Darzin stayed well behind him, idling in a doorway when Pron stopped in the mouth of an alley. He seemed to be talking to someone. *Bookkeeper Freldt Saymak?*

Pron entered the alley. Darzin eased up to the alley's corner and peeked around it, in time to see Pron turning into a side street.

Darzin followed as closely as he dared.

As he came out of the side street, Pron turned another corner, still in pursuit of the Bookkeeper, Darzin assumed.

"District Criminal Investigator." A Wandering Tribeswoman, covered with flounces and ribbons, rustled up to him in a welter of bulging bags.

"My apologies, Unknown Female Wanderer," said Darzin, with the graciousness which made his manner a byword in the force. "I'm pursuing a suspected criminal; possibly, even now, in the commission of a crime. Please call an officer to attend to your case. Feel free to tell them I sent you."

He feared the distraction would cause him to lose his man but, when he reached the end of the street, he saw Pron down the way, closing the door of a two-story hovel behind him.

~*~

Gord Pron listened at the street door of the two-story hovel until he heard a door upstairs open and close. Then he slipped in and up the stairs. He heard water being run into a pan. The preparation of refreshments; the man planned on a lengthy tryst, then, as the Stokk had supposed. Pron couldn't say much for the man's arena, but perhaps the refreshments would make up for it. If they didn't— Pron wouldn't want to be in that man's shoes if they didn't.

Pron eased back down and out, and hurried away to make his report.

~*~

Darzin stopped to consider. This wasn't any of Innkeeper Boktu Jippir's real estate. Had Pron followed Bookkeeper Freldt Saymak into her own home? Surely Bookkeeper Freldt Saymak lived in better quarters than this.

The Unknown Female Wanderer crackled and bumped up beside him. "District Criminal Investigator," she said, "I don't need to look for an officer. *I* want to help *you*."

Darzin looked at the Tribeswoman with surprise and gratitude. Investigators had always found Wanderers to be as cooperative any other sociotype, but rarely did any citizen chase a copper down the street with offers of assistance.

"Perhaps you can," he said. He looked back at the house. Pron stepped out, slamming his fists into each other in a Stokk expression of gleeful satisfaction. "You see that house? The one the Stokk just came out of?"

"Yes, I—"

"Will you see if you can get in? See if there's a woman in there, with light brown skin, medium brown hair, wearing a double-breasted lilac jumpsuit with a plaid peplum. Just see if she's there. If she is, and she's safe and well, leave her alone and wait for me here. If she's hurt or in danger, notify the station house. Will you do that?"

"Yes, I—"

"Good. Thank you, Unknown Female Wanderer. I only wish there were more around like you."

Darzin let the Stokk Gord Pron pass on the opposite side of the street, then crossed over and resumed the tail.

~*~

Connell Morgan closed the street door of his hideout (or, as he preferred to think of it, his headquarters) behind him.

The big spender was getting heavy. He had carried her this far in his arms, her head tucked against his shoulder. He had cast eloquently sorrowful glances at her dangling legs when anyone seemed to wonder why she wasn't walking, and murmured, "Poor girl. Poor, dear girl."

Now he had no need of pretense, and there was a stairway ahead.

"Allez-humph!" He flopped Bel over his shoulder like a sack of meal. He hoped she wouldn't come around while being treated so disrespectfully or, worse yet, die.

Her head hadn't bled at all, but her color had gone bad. Morgan unlocked the door of his rooms with a trembling hand and double-locked and barred it on the inside.

He dumped Bel on a divan and felt her skull. He found a lump the size of a hen's egg.

She's all right. I think she's all right. I hope she's all right.

He went to a sink in the corner of the room and ran cold water into a saucepan. He dropped a rag into the pan and went to minister to his captive, gathering up a length of cord on his way. She had almost brained him in the alley. She'd be dangerous, loose.

If she lived.

Morgan came very close to praying. *What on Earth— What on Llannonn would I do with a corpse?*

Chapter 9

Rewind. Change angle. Replay scene.

Tetra Petrie was enjoying her liberty, though she would have enjoyed it more if she'd had someone to share it. Not Quatro, who was certified NDF: No Damn Fun.

She thought she might try to talk to Bel Schuster, but Schuster latched onto Wotan Hessaphess, of all people, and seemed to be trying to get him drunk.

Tetra could have saved her the trouble. Hessaphess could drink Tsung Li under the table, and not even Tetra could do that.

After a while, Schuster moved, and Tetra gathered her gall to push in where she might not be wanted. But Schuster moved again, and fell into a card game with a native woman. Tetra gave up the project.

The other members of the shore party chattered in animated conversation with several Llannonninn, with much loud talk and bursts of laughter. Tetra wanted to join them, but all the tables were filled.

A Llannonninn man came over to Tetra's table.

"May I join you?"

"Please do," said Tetra. "May I buy you a drink?"

"I wouldn't mind," said the man.

They ordered beer, and traded names while they waited for their brews to arrive.

"Tetra Petrie."

"Squanto Uncus."

The name was odd, yet somehow familiar.

He waved a hand at the full tables, ending the gesture with a fillip that included Tetra. "You're down from the ship?"

"Yes."

"Been away from home long?"

"About nine years, not counting the occasional visit."

"Get homesick, do you?"

Tetra shrugged. "Sometimes."

"Well, I'm going to do you a favor." He pulled a five-by-twelve manila envelope out of the inside pocket of his loose-weave suit and put it on the table. "What do you suppose is in there?"

"Letters of transit, signed by General de Gaulle?"

"What?"

"Never mind. I have no idea what is in there. Why do you not tell me, and save us both some time?"

Uncus opened the envelope and pulled out a sheaf of legal-sized papers. Each paper had a holophoto in one corner, was covered with thick paragraphs, and ended with signature blanks.

"Real estate," said Uncus. "Genuine Earthling real estate."

"I am not an Earthling," said Tetra. She pulled aside the scarf which covered her gills, then put it back in place. "Gilhoolie," she said.

"Oh," said Uncus. "I beg your pardon."

"Not at all," said Tetra. "An understandable mistake."

"Perhaps you're still interested."

Tetra shook her head. "But do not run off. Why do you not sit a spell?"

Uncus put his papers away. "Wish I could," he said. "But business calls." He looked around, found all the tourists taken, and left for greener pastures.

Alone again, Tetra amused herself by seeing how many brands of beer she could taste before she could no longer tell them apart.

When that time came, she found the Llannonninn gone from her shipmates' tables. Some of the Unionites had moved to the hologram arcade at one end of the barroom, and the others had regrouped. Still no room for Tetra.

Bel Schuster's card partner left, but Tetra didn't feel up to a snub.

Now that Uncus had brought it up, Tetra *was* homesick. She almost wished Quatro had come down with her, so they could dredge up times past in the jolly old nursery bubble.

She called for a highball glass of water, and dabbled her fingers in it and thought of home. How the images came flooding back! Waiting to take the sub to the library, hoping it would hurry so they wouldn't have to hear Father tell them, yet again, how he had to swim everywhere in his younger days. Playing hooky from their studies, sneaking off to the old walking hole and coming home with the inner seams of their clothing dry, and being sent to bed without their kelp. Sitting around the old ultramarine radio, listening to off-world entertainment on the "Seabottom Home Companion" show.

"Oh, Genevieve," Tetra sang softly, "Sweet Genevieve."

"The days may come," sang Wotan Hessaphess, from the next table, "the days may go."

Another voice, rich in fermentation, joined the song, and then there was a quartet.

Hessaphess and the tenor began a disputation on whether their next number should be "Feelings" or "Melancholy Baby" when Hessaphess's squawkbox pinged.

"And now, a word from our sponsor," said Hessaphess, and got a laugh.

The squawkbox, worn on the wrist, was about the size of a very large watch. Lightweight and streamlined, once you got used to wearing one you hardly noticed you had it on. Everyone from the *Uncle Gus* wore one. Each had a personal call code, or all could be raised at the same time. Squawkboxes were always set to receive; voice-activated to send.

Only Hessaphess's squawkbox pinged now. Only Tetra took any interest.

"You pay attention," her paternal grandmother had taught her, "you learn something."

"Activate," the engineer said, his slackness falling from him like a pair of baggy pants. "Hessaphess here."

Tetra tried to catch the far end of the conversation, but she could only hear a tinny chirping.

Hessaphess looked around.

"Yes," he said. "They're all here. 1215?" He looked at the timepiece over the bar, then at his own. "Right."

Tetra spoke, though Hessaphess was far from her first choice of conversationalists. "Bed-check?"

"Recall." He rose. "Recall, by order of the Captain," he announced. "STAT. Let's go, people."

In the reception lounge, Hessaphess counted noses. Then he counted ears and divided by two.

"Somebody's missing," he said, and looked more closely. "Schuster. I knew it. She's gone off—"

"I saw her in the bar just now," Tetra said. "She must not have heard you."

Not likely, she agreed, but, when you have eliminated the impossible, whatever is left, however improbable, must be the solution.

"Ven Petrie, you have one minute to bring Ven Schuster back here or to return without her. This party is recalled as of 1215. Anyone not with us is ditched. Do I make myself clear?"

"Perfectly clear." Tetra left at a run.

~*~

As Freldt crossed the lobby, the very small woman who had come in with Operative Bel Schuster ran out of one of the reception lounges.

The woman slid to a halt and smiled.

"I was just coming for you. We thought you would not make it. Come on. Hurry!"

"Thought I wouldn't make it?" Oh, yes, this was one of

the operatives. They had been afraid she wasn't going to make it. They had been afraid for her, when *they* were the ones who took all the risks, faced all the dangers. Now these glorious heroes wanted her to come with them, maybe only to make a formal identification, or to fill out a report. Or maybe Operative Bel Schuster had already made an arrest, and they needed her personal testimony to send the criminal Stokk up the river!

"I'm coming," Freldt said. She wished her friends could see her now.

"Thirty seconds," Hessaphess said, when he saw them.

Freldt smiled warmly at him. This was Operative Bel Schuster's Galactic Union contact. "I'm so pleased to meet you, Galactic Union Space Trooper Thirty Seconds," she said. "You've all done a wonderful job here."

"Schuster's round the bend," said the engineer to the company in general.

"I look forward to meeting her again," said Freldt.

Hessaphess activated his squawkbox. "Hessaphess here. Ready to board."

Freldt began to turn, to say something to the very small woman, when the lounge vanished. Instead, they all stood, just as they had stood in the Inn, in a large, bare room with silver walls, floor, and ceiling.

In a corner of the room, a woman and a man were closed in a large glass box.

Freldt couldn't see them well for the light glaring on the glass, but she could guess who they were, and her heart lurched within her.

Tricked! Tricked and trapped! Gord Pron had been too crafty for them. Darzin and his operative stood prisoner, locked in a glass box, while Stokk in disguise had toyed with her, lured her to this place. She should have known, when she had seen their leader was red. And now they had her, and now they knew she had betrayed them.

Freldt began a wail ending in a terrified shriek.

"I knew I should have asked for a psychomedic," said Hessaphess. He put his massive hands on either of Freldt's arms. "Take it easy," he said. "It's all right. You're on the ship."

"On the ship!" Freldt hyperventilated. "On the ship!" Her eyes rolled up under her lids and she collapsed between Hessaphess's hands like a popped balloon.

Chapter 10

Captain Fazzaria relaxed. At least something had gone without a hitch.

Then her squawkbox sounded.

I knew it. Reassuring, in a way.

"Activate," she said. "Fazzaria here."

"Captain, this is Hessaphess. I think you'll want to come to Transfer STAT. Dr. Frazni has been notified."

"Dr. Frazni? Someone's injured?" *Please, let it be that that clown from Hydroponics tried to stuff an olive up his nose. Don't let it be an interplanetary incident.*

"No, Captain, not an injury."

Jinx was never in the mood for Twenty Questions. "Ven Hessaphess, what's happened?"

"It's Ven Schuster. She's run mad."

"Ven Schuster?"

"Yes, Captain."

"Ven Isobel Schuster?"

"Yes, Captain."

"Extra-Terrestrial Humanities and Value Systems?"

"She's the one, Captain. She's become a raving lunatic."

Become?

Jinx had once had a palm tree. In the tradition of so many Captains before her, she had made the care and feeding of it a part of the duty roster. She strongly suspected, but could never prove, Ven Schuster had thrown it into a recycling bin, leaving a note saying "Thus die all tyrants" in its empty pot.

"Captain?"

"I'm on my way. Cease transmit."

Chestney flexed his shoulders. "Trouble?" Always a good guess on the *Uncle Gus.*

"Hessaphess thinks so," said Jinx. "I'm going down to see. You have the conn, Ven Chestney."

Jinx entered the transfer dock to find Dr. Vlador Frazni, the Empathetic Diagnostician and Ship's Medical Director, bending over a supine figure.

Dr. Vlador Frazni, from the planet Bhat, topped out at only 5'3" (Tetra, at 5'2", was the founder and only member of the Make Dr. Frazni Feel Tall Club). With thick white skin and exceptionally large eyes with black irises, he looked like a bald silver marmoset. The cuddly factor was offset by a double row of needle-sharp teeth. When he smiled and suggested that patients do something, they generally did it.

Wotan Hessaphess, the rest of the shore party, and the two transfer technicians on duty stood around doctor and patient, gawking.

"You two," Jinx said to the technicians. "Back to your posts. The rest of you, at ease and back off. Hessaphess, what happened?"

"We transferred down. We went into the barroom, time passed, then you called us back. Schuster sat with me at first; she seemed all right then. She played cards with a local woman for a while, until the local woman left. Schuster didn't come with us when I announced the recall; Ven Petrie went back for her. That's when we noticed something wrong."

"Ven Petrie, what can you tell me about this?"

"Ven Hessaphess has said it all, Captain."

"Did you see her sitting with a local?"

"Yes, Captain."

"Did they eat anything? Drink anything?"

"They drank."

"Could someone have put something in Ven Schuster's drink?"

"Possibly. I observed them casually, not closely."

"I understand."

Dr. Frazni sat back on his haunches.

The Captain touched his shoulder. "Will Ven Schuster be all right?"

"I can only tell you this poor woman is in mild shock. I've countered it the best I can without her active participation. She should be coming around soon, and she should be able to answer some questions. Other than the shock, superficial examination shows her to be in fair general health, perhaps with a slight tendency toward hypertension. As for Ven Schuster, I'd have to examine her to give a diagnosis."

"But isn't this Ven Schuster?"

"It has to be," said Hessaphess. "She bought me a drink."

"I knew it," said Jinx. "I knew it."

The woman who was not Bel Schuster moaned and opened her eyes. Panic settled over her features again.

Dr. Frazni reached down and pressed a spot on her head with one of his three fingers, and the woman's panic reaction faded. She appeared still frightened, but in control.

He spoke with the soothing tone which made even *This will hurt just a tiny bit* sound believable. "Who are you, my dear?"

"No response," said Freldt. "Don't ask. You'll probably be able to force any information you want from me, but you'll have to work to get it. Well, work *some*, you know."

Jinx sat on her heels next to Frazni. "One of our people is stranded on your planet," she said. "Possibly in danger. If you have any information which could possibly help, please tell us."

"No response," said Freldt. "Don't ask. If they're in danger on Llannonn, then good for Llannonn. That's what *I* have to say about it."

Jinx rose. "Ven Hessaphess? Ven Petrie? Any of you?"

Angela Pevsner, a corporal from Navigation, said, "I saw Ven Schuster leave with somebody and come back with somebody. Maybe they switched clothes in the ladies' loo and I didn't notice."

"I thought I saw the woman Ven Schuster was playing cards with leave," said Scott Linker, the clown from Hydroponics. "Maybe it was Ven Schuster who left, instead."

Jinx glared down at the native. "So, the two of you traded places. Why? Whose idea was it? Where is Bel Schuster?"

~*~

Freldt felt herself flushing with joy. She hadn't been completely deluded, then. Operative Bel Schuster, at least, had been genuine. These Stokk were after the operative; they considered the Stokk Gord Pron to be in danger from her. Freldt, by holding out against their bullying and torture as long as she could, could buy Operative Bel Schuster time. She looked to the glass prison in the corner. She gave District Criminal Investigator Pel Darzin and his Unknown Female Operative a look of pride and said, "No response. Don't ask."

~*~

Captain Fazzaria bit a fingernail. What could she do with this woman? She couldn't force her to talk. She didn't dare have Frazni compel her, with drugs or whatever other means he had at his disposal. But she couldn't afford to just shake her hand, apologize for the inconvenience, and send her home. This woman might be a spy, a terrorist. Or she might be an innocent bystander Schuster had suborned for some purpose of her own. At any rate, Llannonn would surely want an accounting of where their citizen had been taken and what had happened to her and why.

Schuster better be in deep trouble. Because, if she isn't, she's going to be.

"Dr. Frazni," Jinx said, "take this woman to sickbay. Make as thorough an examination as necessary to assure yourself she's well and unharmed. Document it." She motioned for two of the shore party to come forward. "Antonioni, Batista, you're with Security, aren't you? Go with Dr. Frazni and Jane Doe, here. When Dr. Frazni's finished with her, escort her to. . . ." *Where?* What might she do? Harm herself? Attack Security?

The cooler seemed uncalled for, but living quarters contained too many potential hazards.

"Quarantine?" Dr. Frazni's suggestion fell on willing ears. "Comfortable, cheery, antiseptic, and, er, uncluttered."

"I see we understand one another, Doctor. Quarantine. VIP treatment, but secure."

"Yes, Captain."

"Antonioni and Batista, I want one of you in the room with her, and one of you outside. You'll be relieved in four hours." Jinx looked at her watch. "That will be 1700."

"Yes, Captain."

Frazni and the Security Troopers helped "Jane Doe" up and out.

"As for the rest of you," said Jinx to the shore party, "I must ask you to consider this entire incident as classified until further notice. I recalled you, you returned to the ship, and that's all you know about it. If I hear one word about any of this on the grapevine — and I would. . . ." Jinx let them each supply his or her own "or else."

"Ven Hessaphess, Ven Petrie, come with me, please."

"Yes, Captain."

"Of course."

"Transfer, ship locus B15, if you please, for myself, Ven Hessaphess, and Ven Petrie."

Ship locus B15 had once been a briefing room. Now, it was called a "clubroom," because the ship's extra-curricular study groups met there. Tetra was Faculty Sponsor of the Rosettastones, the dead language analysis club, and they met in B15. If those bulkheads could only talk, what larks they could recount!

"Now," said the Captain, sitting at the large bulge of a kidney-shaped table. "Be seated."

Hessaphess sat at Jinx's right hand; Tetra, at her left.

"You two seem to have had more contact with Ven Schuster and this Llannonninn we've brought aboard than the others.

Can you think of any explanation for this extraordinary state of affairs?"

"Schuster wanted to go off-limits," said Hessaphess. "So she switched clothes with this native woman and snuck off, planning to get back before time to board."

"Possible. Ven Petrie?"

"The native woman was not wary of me on Llannonn," she said, "nor of Ven Hessaphess. She said we were doing a good job, and she looked forward to meeting Ven Schuster again. Only when she found herself in strange surroundings, specifically when Ven Hessaphess told her she was aboard a ship, did she scream and lose consciousness."

"What does that indicate?"

"I have no idea, Captain. But Llannonn hardly seems temptation enough to seduce Ven Schuster into disobeying a direct order."

"True," said Jinx. "So, what does that leave?"

"Treachery," said Wotan Hessaphess. "Foul play. Murder."

"Mur. . . Mur. . . Murder," said Jinx. "Come now, Wotan, aren't you being melodramatic?"

"Mark my words," he said, not without a certain glum relish.

"Captain, if I may speak out of turn," said Tetra.

"Yes, Ven Petrie?"

"Naturally, you noticed the Llannonninn was not wearing Ven Schuster's communications device."

"Uh, naturally."

"Supposing Ven Schuster retained it, might we not be able to contact her, and demand an explanation from her directly?"

"Excellent idea, Ven Petrie!" Jinx activated her own squawkbox and gave the call number for the communications console on the bridge. "Ven Meichi, see if you can raise Ven Isobel Schuster for me. She's down-planet."

"But, didn't she come aboard with the others?" When

Jinx didn't answer, the Communications officer said, "Yes, Captain."

No explanations. That's the ticket.

Before Jinx could break contact, Ven Meichi spoke again. "Captain, we have a transmission from the Grand Council Chamber on Llannonn. From Councilor Bella Yozgat."

"Head of the Llannonn for the Llannonninn movement," said Jinx. "I needed this."

"Shall I tell her you're in conference?"

"No. I'll take it here in B15."

"Yes, Captain."

"And hold off on raising Schuster until further notice."

"Yes, Captain."

In fact, Jinx realized, this call might be about Schuster. She hoped it was. She hoped it wasn't.

A life-size hologram of Councilor Bella Yozgat appeared in the bend of the table's middle. She could've been the founder and only member of the Make Tetra Petrie Feel Tall Club; she was 4'11", an elegant little scrap. Her lips were thin, or now compressed to thinness.

"Captain Joan A. Fazzaria?" Her low, harsh voice sounded like the crunch of dried leaves played at slow speed.

"Yes," said Jinx. She gave the notice of recording and intention of review she'd given Nyakk, receiving curt nods of acceptance. "Councilor Bella Yozgat, I believe?"

"Captain Joan A. Fazzaria, I felt it my duty to report the atrocious manners of your shore party, particularly of its leader, at the time of its withdrawal."

Jinx looked neither to the right nor to the left, but straight ahead like a Trooper. "You have my sincere apologies."

"An apology will hardly suffice, will it?"

Apparently not.

"Councilor," said Jinx, "our people have been withdrawn from Llannonn. Their manners can give you no further offense."

Except for those of one. Oh, that one!

The rouge on the Councilor's cheeks faded in comparison to her angry flush. "This is the sort of thing I expected. I told them how it would be. Perhaps now they'll believe me."

"I do apologize, Councilor. I'm afraid I don't know what more you expect."

Councilor Thomms Nyakk stepped into the hologram projector next to his fellow Urbanite. "We're all deeply disappointed," he said. "I, perhaps, most of all, since I have been most voluble in support of membership in the Galactic Union."

"You see," Yozgat said to him, "it's quite unthinkable."

"I see nothing of the kind," he said.

Bella Yozgat gave him a look that could strip paint and shouldered him out of the way. "Captain Joan A. Fazzaria," she said, "the Grand Council has voted to give you every opportunity to make amends. My esteemed colleague assured me this rebuke would be sufficient. It appears he was wrong. You have until dek this evening to do the right thing. If you have not done so by that time, we will have no choice but to report your insult to the Galactic Union Ambassador and hope for redress from your superiors. Do I make myself clear?"

"Perfectly clear," said Jinx. *Except I don't have a clue to what you're talking about.*

"Until then, you may consider yourself under interdiction. You may communicate with this body or with Jok'rel's Traveler's Rest Inn, and with no one else on Llannonn. You will not use your transportation mechanism to or from anywhere but the Inn. Am I still clear, Captain?"

"As clear as ever," said Jinx.

Transmission was broken.

The Captain turned to Tetra. "Ven Petrie, perhaps this is a communications failure. Do you speak Llannonninn?"

"I do. Not idiomatically, but my textbook Llannonninn is excellent."

"Good enough. Go talk to . . . our guest in her own language. See what you can find out. I need information."

"I will do my best," said Tetra, and Jinx had to take what comfort she could from that.

Chapter 11

Bel woke enough to know she had a headache. She tried to go back to sleep, hoping it would ease off, but two people were quarreling just outside her quarters, and—

Her eyes flipped open like the headlights of a sporty hovercar. Not her quarters.

She was in a large, dim, shabby room shaped like the state of Utah. There were windows in three of the walls, a door in the wall which had no window, and another across from it in the southwest corner of Wyoming. Light sifted through the cracks of the boarded-over windows and through the half-opened door, so she knew she had either been unconscious for a very short time or for a very long time.

The pain in her head localized: dull, with a sharp core that branched out and spread itself into her eyes.

She was bound, hand and foot.

The man who'd said he wasn't going to hurt her blocked the door between the states, arguing with someone outside.

"No! Don't you understand Allesesperanto? I tell you I don't want any ribbons."

"Maybe you have a lady friend?" A woman's voice whined back at him.

"No, I don't have a lady friend."

"Lady! Do you want a ribbon?"

Bel shouted back at her. "I want a cop!"

"You what a what, Lady?"

The man pulled a coin out of his pocket and gave it to the woman with a hearty laugh. "She wants one, after all. Here. Keep the change. Thank you. Goodbye."

He bolted the door and leaned against it, listening as the

woman's heavy footsteps eased down the stairs. A ribbon several shades darker than his sky-blue eyes dangled from his hand.

When the woman had gone, he turned to Bel and sketched a bow.

"Connell Morgan, at your service."

Bel frowned what she hoped was a terrible frown and said, "You'll regret this!"

Morgan smiled and went to one knee next to Bel's divan. "No, I won't," he assured her. "How's the head?"

"It hurts."

"Thirsty?"

"Among other things."

Morgan lifted Bel into a sitting position. He fetched a glass of buff-colored liquid from the table.

"Drink some of this."

"What is it?"

"A local concoction. Relieves pain, promotes healing. The Wandering Tribes use it, and it seems to work."

Morgan put the glass into Bel's bound hands. She considered dashing the liquid in his face but, although it would be dramatic, and would make a stirring illustration in a graphic novel, she realized it would also be extremely stupid.

So she drank it. It tasted like a vanilla malted with a kick to it.

"Now, just lean back and let it take effect," Morgan said. He took the glass to the table, out of the reach of someone who might possibly want to use it as a weapon.

He looked down at the blue ribbon he still held. "This is yours, isn't it?" He tied it in Bel's hair. "It becomes you. Brings out the gold in your eyes."

He sat next to Bel on the divan. Very next.

Bel absent-mindedly dug an elbow into his ribs until he moved away.

"Was I crowding you? Do forgive me."

The pain in Bel's head eased. "What's your name again?"

"Connell Morgan. My friends call me Connell. I want you to call me Connell, because I want you to be my friend." He turned on the smile. "And you? I mean, I know who you are, but what's your name?"

"My name is Isobel Enid Schuster. My friends call me Bel. I want you to call me Ven Schuster, because I want you to untie me, unlock the door, and drop dead."

"I sense a certain amount of hostility," said Morgan, as if this were an insight.

"That's coming from me, that hostility you sense," said Bel. "People slamming my head upside a wall tend to bring out the worst in me."

"Now, now, my dear young woman, an accident, I assure you! I only wanted to prevent your bashing *my* head in with a club. You should have let go of it. It was more *your* fault than mine you were hurt, you know. I never meant for you to hit the wall; it was purely an unhappy chance. You can hardly hold me responsible for the vagaries of Fate, can you?"

Bel didn't answer.

"Well, can you?" Morgan's eyes opened wide with boyish innocence.

Bel knew that look well from the classroom. It was the sure sign of a scoundrel.

"Tell me why," Bel said at last. "Why? A woman who's just had her money belt snatched is a poor prospect for robbery. And, if you planned to commit a crime against my person, you wouldn't have carried me off to tend my wounds."

"I had no intention of committing a crime against your person," said Connell. "Not my style of thing at all. Good God, what do you take me for?"

"Untie me and give me back my club and I'll show you."

Connell laughed warmly. "I love combining business and pleasure," he said.

"What business? What pleasure?"

"The pleasure," said Morgan, flicking the bow in Bel's hair, "is the pleasure of your company."

He rose and crossed the room. He went to each of the three windows in turn, peering through cracks, apparently at the streets outside. Satisfied, he sat again, this time out of elbow reach.

"I'm an entrepreneur," he said. "I'm not a rich man, but I've done fairly well for myself selling various goods and entitlements."

Bel gave the room another look. "Oh, yeah?"

Connell cleared his throat. "Temporary," he said. "I found it necessary to change my address, and the housing shortage in this city is appalling."

"Uh-huh," said Bel.

"I went to Jok'rel's today to meet some clients, do some civilized business over drinks, when your party came in. I believe Jok'rel has a contract with the Galactic Union: The Inn's always full of tourists, so that was no surprise. But the Trooper came as a bit of a nasty shock."

"Why?"

"Personal reasons which I don't care to go into right now."

"Let's see if I've got this straight," said Bel. "You're a crook. A con-man, probably. It's getting hot for you: so hot, you had to duck out of your rooms. You were at the Inn to see if you could get one more milking before the cow went dry. In walked John Law, in the shape of an Inverdinian in a Trooper's uniform. How'm I doing?"

Morgan opened and closed his mouth a couple of times. "Mind like a laser beam," he said, forcing a smile. "I expected no less. I could hope for no more."

"Couldn't you?"

He shook his head. "Stupid people are hard to deal with," he said.

"Oh, I hope not," said Bel but, perhaps fortunately, Morgan missed it.

"Intelligent people like you, my dear, are quick to grasp the essentials of a situation, quick to understand the alternatives and to weigh them, to choose the least unacceptable, and to comfortably rationalize their choice."

"This is going to be a pip," said Bel.

"The Trooper, as I said, came as a shock. The reason, you've guessed. Then I noticed his companion. You, my dear. He had you firmly in tow. I noticed you did the buying. I noticed you saw to it he did most of the drinking. I saw you slip away from him. I saw you find a woman of your own general description and change places with her. I saw you assure yourself the Trooper took the other woman for you, and I followed you when you made your escape."

"My escape? So, what do you think, I'm a criminal or something? You think the Space Troopers take their prisoners out on a toot before they throw them in stir? You looking for a partner, or what?"

"My dear, you're caught! I'm not mistaken, and I cannot be misled. You're some kind of VIP, traveling under Trooper escort. That wasn't a shore party, but a squad of Secret Service guards. You got tired of it. Heavy rests the head that wears the crown, and so on. You saw your lookalike, and conceived a plan for slipping away and mingling with the plain folk for a while. Unfortunately for you, I'm more alert than your escort, eh?"

Bel thought the man viewed too much adventure fiction, but wisely restrained herself from telling him so. "Very clever," she said. "Very ingenious, but it simply isn't the case."

Suddenly, Morgan didn't look like a man to take lightly. He looked on the verge of fright and, because his fright would be desperate, he looked dangerous. "It *is* the case," he said. "For your sake, it had better be. Because, if it isn't, you would be worse than useless to me, wouldn't you? If you weren't my only hope, you'd be a liability. And, much as it would pain me to do so, I'd have to dispose of you."

"You mean. . . . You wouldn't . . . *kill* a person, would you?"

"Kill?" Morgan put an arm around Bel's shoulders and held her; whether to comfort her or himself, perhaps not even he could have said. This time, Bel's elbow kept its own counsel. "How could you even think such a thing? No, indeed. Not my style of thing, at all. I'd simply sell you to some people I know. Wanderers. If I'm wrong about you, I'll need the money."

"Morgan," said Bel. "Connell. Congratulations. You have penetrated my disguise. I'm not at liberty to reveal my true identity, you understand, but I can tell you this: you are absolutely correct." What would happen now, Bel couldn't begin to guess. She'd just have to take things one lie at a time.

"I knew it. I knew it." Morgan stood and went to a cabinet by the sink. "A drink, to celebrate? I have some whiskey. Not local stuff, but real Kentucky bourbon. Imported by transfer stations to keep it stable. I've been saving it for a special occasion. This qualifies."

"Thank you. I'd be delighted." *Another glass, another weapon. This kookaburra has got to go.*

But Morgan mixed Bel's drink in a flexiglass bulb, designed for zero-gee. "I only have the one glass," he explained. "I liberated a half-dozen of these on my trip out. Waste not, want not, eh, my dear?"

"Very frugal of you, Connell."

Morgan raised his bulb in a toast. "To you, my dear. To your safe return to the security of Trooper escort, and to my liberation from this benighted planet."

Morgan tipped his head back to drink. Bel stuck the tip of her bulb into the seam of one of the divan cushions and drained quite a bit of the liquor into the stuffing. When Morgan looked at her again, she was taking the bulb from her lips.

"That's the girl," said Morgan. "Now, let's deal."

"I want to go back to the Inn," said Bel. "What do you want?"

"Money. Off-planet. Safe conduct elsewhere and immunity from prosecution here or anywhere else."

"Tall order," said Bel. "Too tall, maybe."

"You'd better hope it isn't," said Morgan.

There was a knock at the Wyoming door: one long, two short, two long, a beat, two long.

"You'll see what I mean," Morgan said, and opened the door.

"You weren't at the Inn," said a hoarse high-tenor voice.

"Come in, quickly," said Morgan, and stood aside.

A man slid in. Morgan locked and bolted the door behind him while the man circled the table, staring at Bel.

The man was scrawny, stooped, ratty, mangy, dressed in layers of rags. From under a grimy wide-brimmed hat gray hair straggled, one lock tied with a new pink ribbon. Eyes like smudges of ink seemed to be estimating Bel's cash value, though Morgan had not yet asked them to. He came closer, smiling. Bel saw teeth shaded yellow-to-green, with spots of brown and black.

"This is a friend of mine, my dear," said Morgan. "Ernest Foy, Jr. Foy, this is Isobel Enid Schuster. She's going to help us. If she doesn't help us, she's up for sale."

"My mother's name was Izzabehl," said Foy. "Still is, as far as I know. It would be a pleasure to sell you, my dear. I'm a man of sentiment, you see."

Morgan nodded. "How much?"

"I said 'sell,' not 'buy,'" said Foy. "I'm not in the market, myself. I'll find a buyer for you and handle all the arrangements."

"And charge a fee. No good."

"Can you afford to be particular? I'll tell you what: I'll do it on commission only. Twenty percent of the purchase price, and I'll waive the fee. You can't ask fairer than that."

Force of Habit

The men shook hands, then hooked thumbs, covering deal-making protocol for both Earth and Llannonn.

Chapter 12

Outside, the bag lady sat on Morgan's doorstep, holding out her hand for money whenever anyone passed. Sometimes they gave her something, and she dropped it into one of her bags. Sometimes they shook their heads at her, or ignored her. The bag lady took no notice; she was thinking of something else.

What's going on? Out in the country, everybody kept track of everybody else. But here, everybody seemed to be keeping track of the same person — the man upstairs, the Stokk, the District Criminal Investigator.

The District Criminal Investigator said he was in pursuit of a criminal, but he *would* say so, if he were interrupted in crime himself. Perhaps they were all on the same payroll. It would make things much simpler.

Maybe she had the answer: Maybe the District Criminal Investigator hadn't been following anybody; maybe he knew very well where he was going. And maybe he didn't want the Stokk to know he knew. The bag lady wondered if the DCI had any Wanderer blood; learning more than people think you know was a standard Wanderer move. But why would he tell someone he had probably assumed was honest to report to the station house?

"If," he had said. *If* the woman was hurt. He would want to disassociate himself from the consequences of that, of course.

The bag lady nodded, and dropped another coin into her bag.

~*~

District Criminal Investigator Pel Darzin, happily unaware that he was being slandered and maligned, trailed the Stokk

Gord Pron through the back streets of the city.

Pron apparently had no thought of being tailed, or was too preoccupied to check, or too cocky to care. Darzin wasn't concerned about losing him, anyway; he was pretty sure he knew the Stokk's destination.

As Darzin expected, Pron led him to the part of town devoted to upper-class recreation. There, the Stokk went into Innkeeper Boktu Jippir's members-only supper club and casino, The Jipp Joint.

I was right! He's gone to report to his boss. But what is he going to report? That Freldt had taken refuge behind a locked door? That Freldt had been killed? Disabled? Taught a lesson? And would what he told his boss be the truth? Darzin had enough experience with Stokk to know it might not be.

Whatever the Stokk said, Darzin wanted to hear it.

Darzin slipped into an alley and turned his fuchsia uniform tunic inside out. Now, it was the sort of cheesy green material a Rural might wear to the city. His black shirt and trousers would pass for city-bought finery. A few seconds with his comb, and his hair was parted in the middle and plastered down over his ears, as if he wanted it obvious he intended to let it grow long enough to plait.

Darzin swaggered to the entrance of The Jipp Joint, like a hick who wanted the city to think he measured up to it, and went in.

He was in luck. The Stokk Gord Pron loitered in the entrance hall, talking to a Stokk Female. Darzin knew she was female because of the several grommets in the rims of her ears; this one's grommets glittered with jewel chips and were threaded with fine gold chain. *Pretty expensive ear job for a woman wearing a plain, loose-fitting suit, tight at the ankles and wrists.* Darzin pegged her as one of the club's bouncers.

Darzin stuck his hands in his pockets and stared at the decor like a man who incorrectly assumed he had a right to pass judgment on it. But he kept an eye on Pron.

Pron spotted the "hick" and pointed him out to the bouncer. They both spread their lipless mouths in derision.

"Gotta go," Pron said. "Take care."

Pron and the female punched each other on the shoulders and Pron headed for the rear of the entrance hall while the bouncer headed for Darzin.

"May I see your membership card, please?" The female clearly didn't expect to see one.

"Membership card? What might that 'ere be?"

"I'm sorry, but no one is allowed in the club without a membership card."

"Reckon money'll do," said Darzin.

"Please forgive me, but I'll have to ask you to leave. I may not make any exceptions."

The woman's courtesy was flawless. She'd been well trained. She'd probably been well-trained in more than courtesy. Darzin hoped he didn't have to find out.

He didn't have to. Just as she reached for his arm, the Stokk Gord Pron rapped on a door at the end of the wall to Darzin's left, entered, and closed the door behind him.

That was all Darzin needed to know.

"I'll go, I'll go," he said. "E don't have to get grumpity. E meant no harm; 's just looking."

"Of course," said the woman. "Think nothing of it."

"Money's good most places in this 'ere town," Darzin said, as if determined to save some face. "Reckon I'll spend it where it's wanted."

The woman walked Darzin to the door. She took a slip of paper from a filigree holder on the wall.

"Please accept this from the management," she said. "It's a coupon good for one free meal at the Council City restaurant of your choice. And, if you know any members of our club, please ask to be nominated for membership. Your business would be most welcome. Have a nice day."

The doors of The Jipp Joint closed behind the District

Criminal Investigator. Innkeeper Boktu Jippir knew how to keep the forms, Darzin certainly had to give him that. He tucked his coupon into a pants pocket and went looking for a window into the room Pron had entered.

Darzin found the window in the alley. Finding it didn't do him much good: it was filled in, stuccoed over, and painted with a view of the Great Sand Sea of Stokk.

So much for that bright idea. Not a total loss, though. An honest Investigator could always do with a free meal.

Now what? Ordinarily, Darzin would call HQ and make a full report. *Out of the question, in this case.* If someone on the Grand Council really were involved with Jippir and his schemes, a full report would alert the Councilor and, through the Councilor, the Stokk.

He'd have to call in, though, and let the force know he hadn't gone Wanderer on them.

Darzin spotted a modem booth a couple of blocks away; close enough to see Pron, if he left, but too far for a suspicious mind to immediately connect it to Jippir's establishment. He went in and typed the code for his office.

An electronic voice on the other end repeated the code and said, "Receiving. Please begin."

Darzin typed, identifying himself, the date, and the time. "For private files only," he typed. Realizing even private files can be accessed, he worded his report carefully. "Spotted Subject One leaving contact point, pursued by Subject Two. Kept Subject Two under surveillance until he entered a domicile and left alone. Deputized a citizen to determine well-being of Subject One and self followed Subject Two to his place of business. Unable to infiltrate or overhear anything transpiring there. End of report."

The electronic voice came on again. "District Criminal Investigator Pel Darzin," it said, "please proceed to Jok'rel's Traveler's Rest Inn as soon as possible, by order of the Grand Council. There has been a breach in diplomacy and the presence of the Galactic Union Ambassador may be required. If so, you will serve as the Ambassador's honor guard at the Inn. Please acknowledge."

"Acknowledged," Darzin said.

"Do you wish a printed copy of these orders?"

"Negative," Darzin replied, and broke the connection.

A breach in diplomacy? The presence of the Galactic Union Ambassador? Darzin wished HQ had given him some details, but he supposed this was a "need to know" situation, and there was little HQ felt he needed to know.

What he *did* need to know were the movements of Innkeeper Boktu Jippir and his people. He needed to know what had happened to Bookkeeper Freldt Saymak, and if anyone went in or out of the house he had tracked her to.

He needed somebody he could trust.

Darzin tried to think his way around it, but there was only one thing to do. He'd have to call up The Irregulars.

The Irregulars: a disorganized muddle of ragtag and bobtail volunteers that didn't have enough cohesiveness to be moled or enough enterprise to be corrupted. A friend of Darzin's, an Assistant Librarian in a facility specializing in Old Earth books, claimed they got the idea from a Street Outreach program she had come to regret.

Darzin, still keeping an eye on The Jipp Joint, typed a code into the modem.

A child answered.

"Is Juvenile Orgon Peir there, please?"

"Just a minute."

Darzin waited. The same child came back on.

"Who wants him?"

"I do. Would you put him on, please?"

A moment later, an older child came on.

"This is Juvenile Orgon Peir. What is this?"

"Juvenile Orgon Peir, this is District Criminal Investigator Pel Darzin. Can you get me at least two pairs of eyes?"

"When?"

"Soonest."

"For how long?"

"I don't know."

"Where you need them?"

Darzin gave the addresses.

"What are they looking for?"

Darzin described "Freldt" and Pron.

"Yeah, okay, it's Sixday, lotta people not doing much, sure. You'll be where?"

"Jok'rel's Traveler's Rest Inn."

"I'll put two on each place; one to watch and one to call in reports. What's the number at that Inn place?"

Darzin looked up the number and gave it to young Peir.

"Will do," Peir said. "The Irregulars are on the job."

Chapter 13

Gunjin Boktu Jippir's Stokk employees liked the way he provided the occasional touch of home. Gord Pron did, now, as he entered The Jipp Joint, unaware of the minion of the law upon his heels. He felt good, and there was nothing like the sound of a brass spit gong hit dead center when a fellow felt good.

A female voice said, "Somebody's been up to something."

It was Korp Norstu, The Jipp Joint's top bouncer. Slightly shorter than Pron, she had the tight, cable-like muscles of the precision fighter. Her loose samtal would have hidden any figure she had, if Stokk women had had any figures. She wore thin gold chains in her grommets today. *Very nice.*

She came up from behind Pron and frogged him in the ribs.

"Hey, Beautiful!" Pron grabbed her wrist and twisted it.

She jabbed the inside of his elbow with stiffened fingers and he dropped his hold.

That was one of the things Pron liked about Korp Norstu: she really knew how to flirt.

"Is he in? Gunjin Jippir?"

She nodded. "He said he was expecting you. He's in the office. Ligniss is with him."

"Oh, he is, is he?" Pron frowned. Utrop Ligniss was a strongarm man. Did the Gunjin think Pron couldn't handle the situation alone? Did he think Pron would need extra muscle to deal with this Freldt Saymak? True, she was a bookkeeper, and bookkeepers on Stokk were very ugly customers. You didn't mess with bookkeepers on Stokk.

This wasn't Stokk, though. Bookkeepers on Llannonn were ordinary people, and ordinary people were substandard, to the Stokk mind. Maybe the Gunjin was out of touch. Maybe some of the iron was going out of his grip.

Pron liked that idea. Come to think of it, he also liked the idea of working with Utrop Ligniss. It never hurt to have a buddy who could braid steel, especially if you looked to the future.

"So, are you going to tell me what you're so happy about, or aren't you?"

"A job's going good, that's all."

"When you're on your way to see the Gunjin, that's good enough."

The street door opened and a tourist came in, dressed in a black blouse and trousers and a cheesy green tunic, his hair parted in the middle and slicked down over his ears.

"I'm impressed," Pron said, in Stokk. "Aren't you?"

Norstu clucked her tongue in the Stokk version of a snicker. "Who left the barn door open?"

If this were Stokk, Pron would have stayed to watch Korp Norstu work. On Stokk, when a bouncer bounced you, you really bounced. This being Llannonn, however, a classy guy like Gunjin Jippir expected the locals to be evicted according to local etiquette, which did not include any form of bloodletting.

"Gotta go," Pron said. "Take care."

He and Korp Norstu punched each other on the shoulders and he went to make his report.

The Gunjin's office was at the rear of the entrance hall. Pron knocked, heard the buzz telling him the lock had been disengaged, and entered.

Gunjin Boktu Jippir sat behind a small, lightweight desk, one easy to heft and use as a shield or a weapon, should the need arise. The Gunjin was still that much on the ball, anyway.

Jipper was a deep orange-yellow. He kept his head shaved but, by this time of the afternoon, a turquoise stubble covered his skull. He'd have to shave again before dinner. He was thin, with the heavy jowls of a man who had once been fat. Nobody knew the story behind that. Nobody dared ask.

"Gunjin Pron," said Jippir. "Sit down. Sit down. You know Gunjin Ligniss, I believe?"

Pron nodded at the strongman. Though he was no taller than Gord Pron, his muscles bunched under his skin like the stuffing in an old pillow. His color was a delicate apricot. He wore a russet tunic, like the local Rurals wore, over a gray samtal, everything loose enough to give his muscles full play, but with no flappy bits to catch or be caught.

Ligniss nodded back. "The Gunjin thought you might want some backup," he said. "Do you?"

"It depends on what the Gunjin wants to do when he hears my report."

Jipper grunted. "Is it urgent?"

Pron shook his head.

"Have a drink then. Gunjin Ligniss, get him a drink."

Ligniss went to the bar in the corner of the room and poured Pron a tall glass of something clear.

"*Hedellma*," said Jippir. "From Stokk. I can't see the appeal of this alcoholic slop they drink. Can you?"

"I can take it or leave it. I'd rather leave it."

"Good man."

Pron sipped his *hedellma*.

Jipper watched him, "Good?"

"Great," said Pron. "Just like mother used to make."

"You said you have something to report?"

"Something unexpected came up."

"Let's hear it, then," said Jippir.

"Saymak was waiting for me when a bunch of Galactic Union tourists came in. One of them latched onto Saymak; she couldn't shake her, so she finally left. She waited for me in the lobby, but she warned me not to speak to her there. I followed her, but she ran into an admirer. He knocked her cold and carried her back to his arena."

"You went after him?"

"Naturally. The windows are boarded and he locked the door. We'll know where she is when we want her."

Jippir looked at the ceiling, as if he tasted his words before they left his mouth. "I want her now. I've been more than patient in this matter. My old mother used to say, 'A Stokk once evened a childhood score on his deathbed, and counted his life well spent.' Am I going to have to wait that long to get what I want?"

"No, Gunjin."

"Is the woman going to cooperate?"

Pron tasted his words as carefully as Jippir had done. "We're not giving her a choice, are we?"

Jippir narrowed his eyes in appreciation of the remark. "No," he said. "We're not. What's your next move?"

"If you wanted to wait, we could watch the arena and pick Saymak up when she comes out."

"I do not want to wait. I want her answer this afternoon, and I want her answer to be 'yes.' My 'friend' on the Grand Council wants to see if we can do this without leaving trace or trail. If we can. . . . Gunjins, think of the money, the power, with a 'friend' on the Grand Council working with us."

The two enforcers thought about it.

"The sooner we take Jok'rel's saloon away from him, the sooner we can move on to some real profits. So, no, I don't want to wait."

"Then we'll have to go in," said Pron.

"Go in? Invade an arena?"

Pron shrugged. "They won't be expecting it. I could talk my way in, or Ligniss could take the door down, or we could blow the lock. Ligniss could take care of the admirer, and I could reason with Saymak."

"Do it with bribery, if you can," said Jippir. "She's no good to me dead or disabled."

Pron felt himself tightening up, but he forced his voice to sound calm. "I was thinking in terms of fingers," he said. "But toes might be better. If I only have to threaten, okay, but I can't break fingers and expect her to punch keys."

Jippir nodded. "You're thinking," he said. "I like a man who thinks. I like to have him working for me. Will you need any weapons?"

"Just Ligniss. If they have any weapons in the arena, we'll take and use them."

"And don't forget the admirer. Handle him with care. If he means something to this bookkeeper. . . . Don't give her anything to resent."

"Let her resent it," said Pron. "What can she do, call the officers? She should have gone to them when I put the arrangement up to her. If she called them now, she'd stand trial for not calling them then."

"She can cross us up, somehow," said Boktu Jippir. "She can drag her feet."

"Not with her toes broken, she can't."

Jippir grunted a laugh.

"In fact," said Pron, "it'll make it easier for us if she likes this guy. If she won't take the bribe, we can hurt her a little, hurt him a little, and promise to hurt him a lot if she doesn't do her job fast and neat."

"That's it, then. We have a plan. Get the deal on paper. Then we'll always have something on her. You never know when you might need a good local bookkeeper."

Pron nodded.

"Pick up a contract on your way out. —And, Gunjin Pron. . . ."

"Yes, Gunjin Jippir?"

"Do me a good job."

"I always do a good job," said Pron. He drained his *hedellma*. "Thanks for the drink."

Chapter 14

Bel began to wish she hadn't wasted all that good liquor.

"Wait a minute," she said. "I thought this selling business was 'or else.' We haven't got to 'or else' already, have we?"

"Just covering the contingency," said Morgan. "Events sometimes have a way of moving too quickly for reasoned debate. Better to make arrangements like this in advance, so there's no misunderstanding or hard feelings later. Am I right, Ernie?"

Foy nodded. "Much better." He scratched his throat. "Have you got anything to drink, my boy? I'm as dry as a tail lasher on a pratty drive."

"Local all right?"

"Fine, my boy."

Morgan put a roll of liquor tubes on the table. "Help yourself," he said.

"Always the perfect host." Ernie Foy, Jr. sat at the table and straightened his slumped shoulders. He removed his hat, and his greasy wisps of hair with it. Beneath the hat, his hair was indeed gray, but short and thick and glossy. He put a hand to his mouth and brought it away full of yellow and spotted fronts. His teeth gleamed white.

"What a life," he said. "Playing up to tourists' notions of what a Wanderer should look like. . . . Sometimes I think I'll chuck it and go Urban." He tore a tube from the roll, bit off the tip, and took a sip.

Morgan noticed the bow tied to Foy's false hair. "Where did you get this? From an old Wanderer with ruffles and ribbons all over her?"

"That's right," said Foy.

"Was she outside here?"

"Just outside the street door."

"Watching, do you think?"

"Panhandling. I've seen her around the city for the past couple of years. She's a real Wanderer, all right, up from the country, probably trying to beg enough money to get back. Forget about her. Are you selling or are you not?"

Morgan didn't look inclined to forget about the bag lady.

Bel certainly wasn't. Bel had no doubt the lady who had stopped her outside the Inn to warn her she was being followed was the lady sitting outside Morgan's street door. Had she witnessed the abduction? Was she planning to blackmail the kidnapper? Inform the police? What?

I've got enough crazy people to deal with right here in this room. I'll worry about the crazy people outside when I get to them.

"Our fair captive," said Connell Morgan, "isn't sure she's worth the price I'm asking from the Union." He switched on the lamp and upped the output until the room filled with a crisp white light. It didn't do a thing for the room.

"What are you asking, my boy?"

Morgan sat and twirled his empty liquor bulb like a top. "Money for you and for me. Enough to move along and seed new business ventures. Immunity for me, and passage off the planet."

"Off the planet? My dear boy, why would you want off the planet?"

"I know the penalty for fraud."

"Don't fancy life in the country?"

"No, I do not."

Foy turned to Bel. "What about you? It would be easier to sell you to an Urban Tribe, but I could be persuaded to arrange for something in the sticks. For, say, ten percent of your net income over the next ten years."

"Income? Where does a slave get income?"

Foy laughed.

"She's a tourist," Morgan said. "She really doesn't know. Where we come from, slaves are property. Were, I mean. Slavery is against the law, now."

"If that's how you worked it, I'm not surprised." Foy took another sip of his local drink. "The Wandering Tribes buy and sell people," he said. "Our word for these people is translated into Allesesperanto as 'slaves,' but they aren't considered the Tribe's property. They belong to the Tribe in the same sense all members of the Tribe belong to it. They're expected to work: make things to sell, tell fortunes, train pratties, whatever. They're expected to give a portion of their earnings to the Tribe. The rest of what they earn is theirs. If they're thrifty, and don't earn so much they drive up their own price, they can buy themselves. Understand?"

"I understand." It still sounded less than appealing. It sounded worse than teaching. Bel didn't want to do it.

Foy's eyes, revealed as bright black in the light of the lamp, assessed Bel again.

"Do you have to stare?"

"Sorry, my dear. Thinking about marketing, that's all. You look like an Urban type, but you might do in the country. As for costume, you need to be very tall or very short or very plump to carry off the flamboyant stuff the country Wanderers wear. In the city, though, you can dress to suit your profession. What are you good at?"

"Comparative value systems," Bel said, and considered the monstrous possibility that her studies might actually prove to be practical.

"There might be some money there," said Foy. "Do you think you could construct your own religion? There's always a market for new religions." He scratched his neck again and looked at Morgan. "I might just reconsider," he said. "I might take her off your hands, after all. I haven't done a religion in years, and I'd welcome the change of costume." He looked back at Bel. "So, what do you say, my dear? Would you want to work for Ernest or for Jack?"

"Who's Jack?"

"I am," said Foy. "When I first met my dear friend Morgan, he was selling names. We hit it off from the first, didn't we, dear boy?"

Morgan grinned. "You tried to palm one of my name books," he said.

Foy grinned back. "And you caught me at it."

"Selling names?"

"Earthling names," said Morgan.

"How can you sell names? Names are free."

"Not if you don't know what they are. There's no such thing as a traditional name on Llannonn. They make them up for the sound of them. I offer them the exotic commodity of Earthling names. If the Llannonninn are willing to pay for them, I'm certainly willing to extend them the opportunity."

"I offered to bring in trade on a commission basis," said Foy, "and Morgan gave me a discount on a name of my own. Two for the price of one, in fact. I'm Ernest in town, and Jack in the country. Now, about your price—"

"Boys," said Bel, "I think we can come to some agreement, here. I really think we can. Just let me get a message to. . . er. . . to my private secretary, back at the Inn, and we'll get this ball rolling."

Morgan narrowed his eyes. "Your private secretary? Not the Trooper?"

"No, indeed. Certainly not. We don't want to get the Space Troopers involved if we can help it, do we?"

"You and your secretary are used to doing things. . . shall we say, through unofficial channels?"

"Sometimes that's just the way it's got to be," said Bel.

"Which one's your secretary?"

Which one is my secretary? Good question. This is my comeuppance for not making chums. I'm up a creek, and who knows me well enough to be my paddle? Faline Mahoud, or Brother Theodore, but they're back on Uncle Gus. *Who in the shore party. . . .*

Bel remembered the wink Tetra Petrie had tipped her when she'd handed Bel the liberty notice.

"The short one," Bel said. "In the magenta sweatsuit and the white neckscarf."

"I remember her. Why wasn't she sitting with you?"

"She deserves a vacation, too," said Bel, in a tone of mild reproof.

"Here's where it ends," said Morgan. "What's her name?"

"Tetra Petrie." What did she know about Tetra Petrie? Professor of Linguistics. Known associates: Her brother, Quatro Petrie, and GeoEco Professor Tsung Li. Library records showed her musical taste ran to the old stuff, like Philip Glass and that crowd; her literary taste ran to a wide range of non-fiction works and Catholic instructional materials. Faculty sponsor of the dead language analysis club. She would do. She would have to do.

"Give me some paper," Bel said, "and I'll write a note."

Morgan left the room.

Foy still stared.

"Ven Foy," said Bel.

"Call me Ernie, dear girl. Foolish to stand on ceremony. Will you be buying a name from Morgan, or will you use your own?"

"I'm going home, Ernie. Learn to live with it. I told Morgan to call me Ven Schuster, but you can call me Bel. Do you know why? Because you're going to help me, Ernie."

"And how am I going to help you?"

"You're going to turn this lunatic in, before he gets you into something you can't get out of."

"Lunatic? What do you mean?"

"He still hasn't told you what this is all about, have you noticed?"

He hadn't noticed.

"He's decided I'm a Galactic Union Department Chief or something, and he's asking for all this money and everything."

"And, if he's wrong," said Foy, "if he can't get all this money and everything, he'll sell you. He's told me that much in plain language, and I'm for it."

Oh.

"Well, when I called him a lunatic," said Bel, "I meant to say he's right. I am Something in the Union. And the Union isn't going to let some penny-ante name-peddler put the arm on one of Us and then just let him walk. Do you hear what I'm saying?"

"I hear you," said Foy.

"Are you thinking about what you can do about it?"

Foy nodded as Morgan came back into the room.

"Here you are," Morgan said. He put several sheets of white paper and a pen on the table.

"You'll have to untie me," said Bel.

"Only your hands," said Morgan. He sat on the divan and began working at the knots binding her wrists. "I'll carry you to the table."

"I'm too heavy. I wouldn't want you to strain anything."

"I carried you here," Connell said. "If I can carry you ten blocks, I can carry you to the table."

He grunted as he lifted Bel. She wondered if she could poke him in the eye, untie her ankles, knock the Wanderer down, unlock the door and make a getaway before either of the men could stop her. She decided she probably couldn't.

Morgan put her in the chair across from Foy and stood behind her. "No tricks, now," he said. "No secret codes, or any such nonsense."

"Secret codes? My dear fellow, people of my stature don't deal in secret codes."

Too true, but there was no time like the present to start.

"Could I have a refill on that bourbon? I write better when I'm lubricated."

"Certainly, my dear."

"Do you have any mixers? Soda, or bitters, or fruit or anything?"

"You want a mixed drink?"

Bel smiled. "I'm just an Old-Fashioned girl," she said, with a mighty bat of her eyelashes. "By the way, have I asked you to call me Bel?"

"Why, no, you haven't."

"Well, call me Bel." She pulled a face at Foy, one wise guy to another behind a sucker's back.

"I'll see what I can find," said Morgan. He turned to rummage in his pantry.

By the time he handed her a bulbful of amber clouded with maraschino cherry juice, she was ready to write.

"I've waited to start," she said, "so you could watch and see I don't try to slip in a secret message. I know I couldn't fool you, Connell, and I wouldn't want you to think I'd even try."

Morgan preened his mustache and sharpened its points.

"Tetra:" Bel wrote. "Emergency! Now the wonderful exotic little vacation's exploded! Bagged looking over city. Knocked silly. Finagle ransom, or my identity nears nonexistence." She signed it I.S. Rosettastone.

"What do you mean," Connell asked, "about your identity? And didn't you tell me your name's Isobel Enid Schuster?"

"Extra impetus," Bel said. "They might hustle if they think my cover might get blown."

"Ah."

"As for the name, now *that's* a code. Only I know to put that at the end of a message. Without it, she would know something's wrong."

"My dear," said Morgan, "you are as clever as you are beautiful."

If so, I'm in deep trouble.

Morgan folded the paper and gave it to Ernest Foy, Jr. "Take this to Jok'rel's," he said. "Someone may have seen me following her; I don't dare go. Give it to the woman she described: she's about so high, sitting with a group of tourists. One of them's a Space Trooper."

"There aren't any tourists at Jok'rel's," said Foy.

"In the bar," said Morgan. "Two or three tables of them, unless they've spread out."

"I just came from there," Foy reminded him. "The officers were clearing the ground floor. A shore party from a Galactic Union ship pulled out early and all but spit in Jok'rel's face. Naturally, he complained to the Council, and the Council's threatened to call in the Union Ambassador."

"They pulled out?" Bel thought she must have heard wrong. She *must* have heard wrong! "They pulled out?" Foy nodded, and Bel said, "They pulled out?"

"Perhaps you're right," Morgan said. "Perhaps you aren't as valuable a hostage as I'd hoped."

"Wait a minute," said Bel. "Ernie, did you hear if the ship's gone, or just the tourists?"

"They say the ship's still up there. Nobody knows why it hasn't left, or why they pulled out, or why they did it with such contempt, or anything besides what I already told you."

"See if you can find out any more," said Morgan.

"I'm an old man," Foy complained. "My old bones. . . ."

"Blast your old bones! Go see if you can find out any more."

"When you say, 'The officers were clearing the ground floor,'" said Bel, "did you mean officers of the law?"

"Yes, of course."

"I can see why you wouldn't want to go, then," said Bel. "Officers of the law arrest people, don't they? Criminals, I mean? If they hear about somebody doing something illegal, and they know where they can put their hands on such a person, they go and get such a person and take him away? Or her, as the case may be? That's the way it works at home, isn't it, Connell?"

"That is undoubtedly the way it works at home," said Connell, with the look of a man who ought to know. "But don't worry about Ernie. He knows how to avoid and evade, don't you, Ernie?"

"I'm the best, my dear," said Foy, putting on his hat and recapping his teeth with a click. "Never fear me."

"Still," said Connell, "she may be right. No sense taking any chances at this point. If the shore party is gone, it's gone, and no amount of information will change that blunt fact. I'm sorry, Bel, but it's the Wandering life for you, after all. Shall I tie her up again, Ernie?"

Bel clutched her wrists, felt her forgotten squawkbox, and abandoned all hope of sliding out of this thing discretely. Let them court martial her, or whatever the Space Troopers did to civilians who disregarded Captain's directives. She'd rather do twenty in Juliette than ten-plus here.

"I have a better idea," she said, and hoped she told the truth this time.

Chapter 15

"But, Tetra," said Quatro Petrie. "Don't you think you should have cleared it with the Captain before you told me all this? Sensitive, highly classified information—"

Ordinarily, Tetra refrained from interrupting Quatro's speeches, preferring to let him drone on while she employed the time with thoughts of her own. But desperate times call for desperate measures, and she interrupted him now. "Do you know what the students call you, Quatro? What everyone calls you, since someone came up with it in the corridor one day?"

"I'm not interested in the feeble jests of the semi-literate," said Quatro. "What do they call me?"

"Pete the Clam," said Tetra. "Because of your reticence. It is legendary. The Captain would not object to my telling you something she does not want spread around. And your assistance is required, not to say essential. Now, just do as I instructed you, and then you can get back to your cross-sectioning."

The Gilhoolies were in sick bay. Tetra had dragooned Quatro immediately after leaving Captain Fazzaria in Clubroom locus B15.

"Dragooned" was the appropriate word: Tetra had taken Quatro to sick bay by way of the commissary. There, she had picked up two yards of gold bric-a-brac and a tube of quick-dry glue. Behind the closed doors of Dr. Vlador Frazni's office, she had cut the bric-a-brac into strips of various lengths and glued the lengths to Quatro's clothing.

"Remember," she said. "Very soft-spoken. Very gentle. Restrained."

"Should I smile?"

Quatro had a smile, which he, following his sister's lead, practiced in front of a mirror, and used in the classroom when pointing out pupils' deficiencies and flaws. He labored under the delusion that it put the students at ease.

Tetra had seen this smile, and had seen young persons whom it had stricken. "By all means," she said.

Now she led Quatro to the quarantine rooms. She gave Batista his lines and had him change places with Antonioni.

Inside Freldt's quarantine room, Batista pretended to wipe a dew of fear from his brow.

"I pity you," he said.

Freldt looked up from her viewscreen. She put the show on pause and took the translation plug out of her ear. She needed a break just now: Bambi stood at the edge the Big Meadow for the first time and the tension was nearly unbearable.

"The Captain has some questions and she wants some answers for them," Batista said.

"No response," Freldt said. "Don't ask."

"I'm not asking. It isn't my job to ask. Asking is somebody else's job."

The door opened, and Quatro came in dressed in khaki trousers, now with gold bric-a-brac down the outside seams, and a red turtleneck, now with gold trim around the neck and cuffs. He wore his favorite off-duty wig, one of short curls the color of weak apple-cinnamon tea. It set off the blue-green of his eyes, though he would have eaten worms before admitting such a thought ever occurred to him.

Batista shrank from him. "Quatro!"

"Leave the room," said Quatro, very soft-spoken, very gentle, restrained.

"My orders—"

"Your orders are to leave the room, Ven," said Quatro. "Now leave, before I take the trouble to remember your name." Quatro was no actor, and he spoke without inflection. The effect was chilling.

"She isn't to be left alone."

"But she won't be alone, will she? I'll be here to keep her company. I'm sure we'll find something to occupy our time."

And he smiled.

Batista left the room.

"No response," said Freldt, with considerably less emphasis than before. "Don't ask."

Quatro only looked at her.

Freldt felt cold sweat popping out in places no sweat of any temperature had ever popped before.

"The Captain thinks you don't answer our questions because you don't understand Allesesperanto," Quatro said. "Do you understand Allesesperanto?"

"Of course I do."

"Good. I hate it when I get impatient with someone, and lose my temper, and then find out they simply didn't understand the question. Especially when it's too late for me to apologize."

He crossed the room to Freldt and took the viewer out of her hand. She gave it up to him, avoiding his touch and scrunching away from him into the corner of her bed. He pressed a button, and the viewscreen went dark.

"A sad show," Quatro said. "They kill his mother."

Before Freldt could scream or faint or otherwise disgrace herself, the door opened again and Tetra came in.

Tetra charged across the room and inserted herself between Freldt and Quatro. She glared up at him, fists on hips, elbows out like the wings of a guardian angel.

He met her glare impassively. "What are you doing here?"

"You are not permitted to question anyone without a witness," said Tetra. "Look at the poor woman. She is afraid."

"Go away, and she won't be afraid for long," said Quatro.

"I will not go away," said Tetra. "I will stay here until you leave, or until she answers the Captain's questions, but not before."

Freldt uncurled a bit at this.

"The woman is hiding something," said Quatro. "That's dangerous. It could get her hurt. I'm not leaving here, whether you do or not, until I know what it is." He smiled again. "I care," he said.

"Then go stand by the door," said Tetra. "She could not answer if she wanted to, with her teeth chattering."

Quatro went to stand by the door.

Tetra sat on the edge of Freldt's bed and addressed her in Llannonninn. "There, there," she said, patting Freldt's chill hand. "Do not be afraid. No one is going to bother you. I will see to it."

"Oh, thank you! Thank you! Who is he?"

"A person of much less importance than he thinks," said Tetra, marveling at how often art imitates life. "The Captain will be upset when she learns he has been hectoring you."

"She will?"

"Certainly. We of the Galactic Union pride ourselves on our courtesy and kindness. That is why the Captain was so surprised when the Council—"

"The Galactic Union?"

"Why, yes. Who did you think we are?"

Freldt stared into Tetra's face. She touched Tetra's lips, ran a finger around their rims, grasped the upper one, and twisted.

"Ouch!" Tetra jumped back from the bed, rubbing her mouth.

"What the blazes did you say to her?" Quatro's voice was harsh with concern.

"You *are* Galactic Union!" Freldt switched back to Allesesperanto. "I thought you were Stokk! Wearing false lips, to fool me. I must have been right all along! You *are* working with District Criminal Investigator Pel Darzin. Operative Bel Schuster *is* part of your group. And, if you really don't know where she is, she's in danger from the Stokk."

"What Stokk?"

"The one who followed her out of Jok'rel's. —Oh, but I forgot the agent who followed them both. He'll look after her, won't he?"

"Agent? District Criminal Investigator? Operative Bel Schuster? . . .Perhaps," said Tetra, "you had better begin at the beginning."

"Why don't you just call the Station House? They can tell you more than I can."

Tetra surreptitiously crooked a finger at Quatro, who stepped closer.

"It all started. . . ," said Freldt.

~*~

"They call it what?" Quatro and Tetra hurried down the corridor toward a transfer alcove, Quatro stripping himself of insignia as they went along.

"The old Mutt-and-Jeff," said Tetra. "The good-cop/bad-cop routine. One person comes on strong and scary, the other one comes on warm and reassuring. It is generally successful."

Quatro nodded, and gave his sister's shoulder a consoling pat. "You can be the good cop next time," he said.

~*~

The Captain assembled a Crisis Team in Clubroom locus B15. It consisted of herself, Dr. Vlador Frazni, Tetra and Quatro Petrie, Wotan Hessaphess, and First Mate Harry Chestney.

"As I suspected," Tetra said, "Ven Schuster did not willfully disobey the liberty restriction. She merely changed clothing with the Llannonninn Freldt Saymak, possibly for a joke."

"For a joke?" Quatro said, permitting himself a faint trace of disgust.

"It is a manifestation of humor," said Tetra.

"I know—"

Jinx waved a hand, and Quatro clenched his teeth in silence.

"Continue," she said to Tetra.

"If I might offer an assumption, I assume the Stokk is responsible for Ven Schuster's disappearance."

"Stokk," said the Captain. "The race that gives a new meaning to the term, 'cut-throat capitalism.'"

"As for the 'agent' Ven Saymak claims put Ven Schuster under observation," said Tetra, but she couldn't finish the sentence, for she hadn't anything to finish it with.

"An Earthling, she said," said the Empathetic Diagnostician. "What made her think so?"

"She said he walked Earthling," said Tetra.

"Captain," said Harry Chestney. "Request permission to transfer down with a Security squad. We'll turn the town inside out until we find her."

"Permission denied."

"But, Captain, a woman needs our help! One of ours! She may be in deadly peril, even as we speak!"

Purple tears welled up in Dr. Frazni's big black eyes. Two thick drops oozed down the white skin of his cheeks and dripped into the terrycloth collar of his lab coat.

"I am not unaware of that fact, Ven Chestney," said the Captain. "But please remember we are interdicted. We have fences to mend before we can even consider mounting a rescue effort. Ven Petrie, what can you tell us about our misstep?"

"I asked Ven Saymak what we had done wrong. She told me what we should have done. As I only know what I heard, and not what Ven Hessaphess may have said or done otherwise, I will leave it to him to judge in what way and to what extent we may have fallen short of expectations. We had contracted to spend twelve standard hours in Jok'rel's Traveler's Rest Inn. We, in fact, only stayed for two."

"Two hours, fifteen minutes, to be precise," said Chestney.

Tetra did not inform him he'd obviously mistaken her for someone who cared. Tetra was above such remarks. "At the time of our early departure," she said, "we should have apologized to Jok'rel for leaving sooner than our contract stipulated, given him our reasons or apologized for being unable to give him our reasons while assuring him they were compelling, and negotiated and paid him a compensation for the loss of ten hours of our business."

"And how far short of this did we fall?"

Hessaphess felt his cheeks burning, but the blush didn't show through the natural raspberry of his skin. "We left."

"A considerable gap," said Jinx.

"Yes, Captain."

"Hardly surprising the Grand Council was shocked," said the doctor.

"One wonders," said Quatro, "why we weren't briefed on protocol."

"Barroom etiquette may not be considered within the purview of Union diplomacy," said the Captain. "Perhaps it will be, when I've made my report."

"Captain," said Tetra, "it seems to me this Jok'rel, who has a standing contract with the Union, ought to know by now the kind of blunders he can expect from tourists. It seems to me, he would have found a way to let us know what we ought to do, or make allowances for our ignorance, unless, of course—"

"Unless," Dr. Frazni said, "he thought we knew, and that the insult was deliberate."

"Bella Yozgat," said Jinx, "arranged for our restriction to the Inn. Suppose she told him we'd been briefed on behavior, although we hadn't."

"Begging your pardon, Captain," said Chestney, "but it wasn't Councilor Yozgat who urged us to pull out early. It was Councilor Thomms Nyakk. And we only have his word for it Councilor Yozgat arranged for the restriction."

Tetra cleared her throat. "Councilor? As in 'Grand Council'?"

"Yes," said Jinx.

"Freldt told me Investigator Darzin suspects someone on the Grand Council of working with the Stokk. Perhaps one or both of these Councilors deliberately sabotaged our shore leave, in order to drive the thin end of a wedge between Llannonn and the Galactic Union."

Hessaphess said something disapproving in Inverdinian.

"What's our next move, Captain?" Chestney flexed his shoulder muscles.

Jinx picked a chip of nail from her tongue. "Suggestions?"

"You people have a saying," said Quatro. "'Discretion is the better part of valor.' Perhaps our best course would be to have Dr. Frazni disguise or remove all memory of this episode from the Llannonninn female's mind, return her to Jok'rel's, and strategically retreat."

"And compound the outrage the Llannonninn feel we've committed?"

"Apologize before we leave," said Quatro. "It needn't take long. You could call this Jok'rel, apologize, negotiate the settlement, and then retreat."

"'Retreat'?" Chestney looked as if he were trying to place the language those sounds represented. "'Retreat'?"

Dr. Frazni raised a hand and spoke softly. "Aren't we all forgetting something?"

"Not all of us," said Tetra.

"We aren't forgetting Ven Schuster," said the Captain, "if that's what you mean."

"I simply suggest, perhaps, we should," said Quatro.

"No," said Tetra.

"At any rate, Captain," said Hessaphess, "we all seem to agree the first thing to do is for you to transfer down and make peace."

"*I* transfer down? The Captain of a Space Trooper vessel, deal face-to-face with an innkeeper? That wouldn't do much for our status, would it? Besides, *you're* the one who insulted him."

Hessaphess wasn't about to go, not unless Dr. Frazni could disguise or remove the memory of his carouse from the Llannonninn Innkeeper's mind. "But I'm only an engineer."

"Since when do you modify 'engineer' with 'only'?"

"I'll apologize," said Chestney. "While I'm at it, I'll find out why he didn't provide us with the rules of the house, whether we were supposed to know them or not." Chestney's jaw shifted from firm to truculent.

"Perhaps someone else," said Jinx. "You're my First Officer, after all. If there should be any danger, you couldn't be spared."

Her eyes focused on Tetra.

"I cannot be spared, either," said Tetra.

"Permit me," said Jinx, "to refer you to the last line of your job description: 'And other duties as assigned.'"

Tetra was reaching for her union card when the Clubroom's intercom pinged.

"Captain," said Ven Meichi, "I have an unauthorized transmission from Llannonn. It's from Ven Schuster. I just thought you ought to know."

"Of course I ought to know," said Jinx. "Put her through."

Ven Meichi hesitated. "The call isn't for you, Captain," she said. "It's for Tetra Petrie."

Chapter 16

It was a desperate Bel Schuster who made the call, and an even more desperate Tetra Petrie who took it.

Tetra seldom upbraided herself. She seldom had reason to. She did it now. *It's my own fault. I had to wink, didn't I?*

Jinx turned to Tetra with "Say it ain't so," written all over her face.

"I am here with Captain Fazzaria, Ven Meichi," said Tetra. "I will just transfer to my quarters."

Jinx tapped the conference table in front of Tetra. "Here."

"I will take it here."

"Through the Clubroom intercom," said the Captain. "Donna, monitor, and see if you can locate the point of transmission."

"Yes, Captain," said Ven Meichi.

The next voice heard in locus B15 was Bel Schuster's.

"Tetra? Is that you?"

"Yes."

"Am I ever glad to hear your voice! Are you alone?"

The Captain, with an evil twist to her mouth, nodded.

"Er," said Tetra.

"If you aren't alone, get alone. This is for your ears only. Classified Super-Hush, understand?"

"Er," said Tetra.

"Your ears and Jinx's, understand? Captain Fazzaria must not know, but Jinx'll have to, because he. . . . Well, I don't have to tell you about *him*."

Jinx Fazzaria looked around, as if to assure herself she hadn't slipped into some alternate universe while her mind was distracted. She pressed the "mute" pad on her com-console. "Go along with it. Either she's trying to tell us something or she's got peanut butter on her star charts. Play along with her."

Tetra nodded, and the Captain released the "mute" pad.

"No," said Tetra, "you do not have to tell me about Jinx. He is here with me now. He sends you all his love."

Bel's sigh thundered and hissed through the com circuits.

A voice could be heard in the background, saying, "Get on with it. You can chat when we're all out of this."

"I'm going to read a prepared statement," Bel said. "I'll call again later. We can't stay on the air long, or the Communications Monitors will pick us up."

A paper rattled, and Bel read the note she had written: "'Tetra: Emergency! Now the wonderful exotic little vacation's exploded! Bagged looking over city. Knocked silly. Finagle ransom, or my identity nears nonexistence. I. S. Rosettastone.' Do you copy?"

"I have it," said Tetra. "What is the ransom?"

The background voice came forward. "Just get the law out of Jok'rel's. We'll be in touch."

The connection ended.

Jinx raised Donna Meichi. "Any luck locating the call's origin?"

"Negative, Captain. It came from Council City, but the call was too brief to get a bead on."

"Thank you, Ven Meichi. We expect another such call. Stand by to boost sensor power and engage locus lock-on."

"Yes, Captain."

Silence fell in Conference Room B15.

After a moment, Jinx prompted them. "Anyone?"

"Peanut butter," said Hessaphess. "On her star charts."

"On the contrary," said Quatro. His recent foray into duplicity had whetted in him a hitherto unsuspected appetite for it. "She was sending us a heavy-handed message saying she's in trouble."

"We know she's in trouble," the Captain pointed out gently. "If we hadn't known it already, her calling from off-limits would have given us a subtle clue, don't you think? Not to mention the fairly straightforward text of her prepared statement and the presence of an apparent captor."

Quatro's face took on a pinched look, the corners of his mouth turned sharply down, which Tetra knew meant he had been touched on the raw.

"Captain," she said, "I believe Quatro is correct. We are missing a subtlety which *he* has observed. Since it is obvious Ven Schuster is in trouble, why did she call our attention to an overlying peculiarity about the call?"

"Peanut butter," Hessaphess muttered, and chuckled.

Quatro nodded. "She wanted us to look more closely at her prepared statement," he said, his confidence restored. "Depend upon it, there's a message hidden there."

"Let's all get out our decoder rings," said Hessaphess.

Jinx simply turned to him, saying nothing, but drumming the tips of her bitten nails on the table.

He subsided.

"May I ask the computer to give us transcriptions?" Tetra's finger rested on the *print* button.

"Excellent idea," said Fazzaria.

"Captain," said Chestney. "Request permission to call up a Security squad to transfer to Ven Schuster's locus as soon as it's determined. We could have her liberated and back aboard ship before the natives know she's raised us."

"Permission denied," said Jinx. "Ven Chestney, you will oblige me by suppressing your desire to storm the fortress before we've established the existence of one."

Harry ducked his head with the half-flattered chagrin of a man certain everybody else secretly envied his impetuosity.

When each member of the Crisis Team had a copy of the contact transcript, Tetra said, "I believe Quatro is right. Ven

Schuster wanted us to examine the prepared statement more closely. That is why she signed it as she did, and why she included the signature with a verbal transmission. 'I.S.' Her initials, of course, and 'Rosettastone,' to indicate a code. And that," she said to the Captain with a dizzying rush of relief, "is why she called me, specifically. Because I am faculty sponsor of the Rosettastones, and would be the person most likely to recognize the indication."

"She reckoned without me," said Quatro.

"Thank you, Mr. Bond," said Tetra, but Quatro was too engrossed in the problem to hear her.

"She wouldn't have had time to come up with something elaborate," said Dr. Frazni. "Especially if, as she says in the text, she was 'knocked silly.' I'm inclined to believe the words of the text are, on the surface, accurate. After all, her captor would know if they weren't."

"Good thinking," said Jinx. "The word choice sounds stilted, though. 'Now the wonderful exotic little vacation's exploded.' 'Exploded'? 'Identity nears non-existence'?"

Tetra took a mechanical pencil from the pocket of her sweatpants and marked some of the message's letters. "Well, I will be a monkey's uncle," she said. "You have hit upon the key, Captain."

"I have?"

"She chose her words partly for their surface accuracy, but also for their initial letters." Tetra read from her paper, "'Ten twelve blocks from Inn.' Ven Schuster has not only told us what happened to her, but her general location. She is within a ten-to-twelve-block radius from Jok'rel's."

Jinx raised ComSpec Meichi again and told her how far to narrow her next scan.

"Shall I collect a squad now, Captain?" Chestney half-rose.

"When I want you to collect a squad," said the Captain, "I'll ask you to collect a squad. I want to know where Schuster is. I may not be able to use the information, but I want to have it. In the meantime, we need to clear and secure the Inn."

"We're bowing to the Stokk's demands?"

"I don't see why we shouldn't," said Jinx, "since he demands we do what we were about to do anyway."

"He does?"

"In effect. Ven Petrie, prepare to transfer to Jok'rel's. I'll have Faline Mahoud cut a credit voucher for. . . . How much do you estimate twelve hours of our custom would have been worth? Anyone?"

Quatro scratched figures on his transcript. "Twelve in the party. . . less one, because Hessaphess never spends his own money. . . times twelve hours. . . times what Tetra spent on Riga. . . less two hours and fifteen minutes. . . . Approximately 340 credit units, Captain."

"Three hun—" She cocked an eye at Tetra.

"Moderate, Captain," Tetra said. "My expenditure on Riga was, as ever, moderate."

Jinx raised Commissariat Faline Mahoud. "Cut me a credit voucher payable to Jok'rel's Traveler's Rest Inn," she said. "For 340. . . . Better make it an even 350 credit units. Send it to locus B15 for signature and disbursal."

"Yes, Captain."

"And prepare the paymaster to garnishee it, five credits per packet, from Wotan Hessaphess's pay."

"Yes, Captain."

Hessaphess blanched to a delicate rose. Jinx got Donna Meichi on the com. "Put me through to the Grand Council," she said.

"Right away, Captain."

"Shall I change clothes?" Tetra indicated her outfit.

"Perhaps it would be best," Captain Fazzaria said. "Something soothing and apologetic. Something dignified, yet penitent."

"I have just the thing," said Tetra.

The intercom pinged. "Captain, I have Councilor Bella Yozgat of the Grand Council."

"Put her through."

The sour-faced Councilor appeared at the bend of the table.

"Councilor Yozgat," said Jinx. "Many thanks for taking my call. We don't deserve such consideration. We are ashamed. Deeply, *deeply* sorry and ashamed of ourselves."

Bella Yozgat's compressed lips sprang apart with an audible pop.

"Coals of fire," Hessaphess whispered gleefully. "Heap 'em on, Captain!"

"I assure you, Councilor," Jinx continued, "our bad behavior was due entirely to ignorance. Thanks to you, we've come to understand our error and we're prepared to correct it."

"How?"

"To begin with, the Duty Officer in charge of the shore party has been severely penalized, and will not be allowed to return to Llannonn, except by the express permission of the Innkeeper himself."

"Don't bother," Hessaphess muttered.

Yozgat nodded. "And?"

"I'm sending my personal envoy to the Inn to apologize on behalf of the party, and to deliver a credit voucher for 350 credit units, the amount of business we estimate Jok'rel's lost because of the recall. We will ask him to hold the voucher for a week. If the shore party is able to return to the Inn within that time, they'll draw against it until it's used up. If they spend over the amount we deposit, they'll pay the difference. If they spend less, he can keep the change."

Yozgat nodded again. "And the reason for the recall?"

Jinx hesitated. "I'm sorry to say I can't reveal the reason, not at this time. Please forgive me. I assure you I would tell you if I were free to do so, and I *will* tell you if I'm ever allowed to."

The Councilor seemed to be looking past the Captain, apparently gathering reactions from Council members out of projector range. After a moment, the Councilor said, grudgingly, "Acceptable. If Innkeeper Knosh Jok'rel is satisfied with your apology and restitution, this body will be satisfied. Will your envoy be arriving immediately?"

Jinx looked at Tetra, who held up the fingers of both hands. "Ten standard minutes," Jinx said.

"We will notify the officers to stand down, for now," said Yozgat. "Frankly, Captain Joan A. Fazzaria, I'm pleasantly surprised. You seem to have acquired an almost native understanding of proper behavior since we last spoke. One might almost think you had smuggled a Llannonninn aboard to advise you."

Jinx showed her teeth and made a sound something like laughter.

"Innkeeper Knosh Jok'rel will be expecting your envoy," Yozgat said. "Until further notice, your ship is still interdicted. Innkeeper Knosh Jok'rel will contact us when this matter is settled and we will contact you. You may transfer your envoy down and, when we say you can, back up. Do you agree with these terms?"

Tetra nodded.

"We agree," said the Captain. "And please let me thank you again for your patience and understanding."

"Yes, yes," said Bella Yozgat, and terminated the call.

"I will go change," said Tetra.

"Ven Petrie," said the Captain, "do I need to tell you not to leave the Inn?"

"I would rather you did not, Captain," said Tetra, and transferred to her quarters.

Chapter 17

"We'll be in touch," said Morgan, and signed off. He kissed the tips of Bel's fingers and released her wrist.

Bel lowered her head. The first hand had gone well, but there were a lot of hands in a deck, especially when everybody was playing a different game and the rules shifted according to who seemed to be winning. That's what Coup d'Etat was all about.

"Well done, my dear," said Morgan. "I dare say they left the Inn because of your loss, and stayed in orbit to demand your return. No doubt they, and not the Council, called for the Ambassador. Foy's muddled it, I expect."

It was obvious to Bel what had happened at Jok'rel's, and equally obvious it wasn't Foy who had muddled it.

Hessaphess, Bel agreed, probably had discovered her absence and pulled the party. Not having done his homework, Hessaphess hadn't known the premium the Llannonninn placed on courtesy and, in his gruff, military way, he had outraged their propriety on the way out. *What a maroon.*

Well, the Grand Council would soon put it right; that's what they were for. At worst, the Ambassador would mediate. Nothing to worry about there.

Meanwhile, Captain Fazzaria would ask the Council for help in finding her missing crewmember. Bookkeeper Freldt Saymak might be able to help the officers, there; she had seen Bel leave, and she had seen Morgan giving them the once-over when they came out of the Female Humanoids' room. Everything had happened so quickly, Freldt Saymak might still be on the spot. If she'd left, Bel felt certain the officers would be able to find her, if they only knew to look.

Bel heard the sound of large hands being rubbed merrily together, then felt one of those hands laid, with a hearty shake, on her back.

"Courage, woman! Cheer up! Things are nicely set in motion. The Troopers will open the Inn for us, and off we'll go! We're as good as off-planet already."

Bel didn't see it happening quite so easily. The Captain would get the Inn open, as diplomatic relations demanded she do, but cut a deal with a criminal for the sake of Isobel Schuster? No.

On the other hand, the Church wasn't known for turning a blind eye when Her people came up missing. Not even the Jesuits rode into town waving crosses and double-edged swords anymore, but they didn't let it slide, either.

Of course, the Church also wasn't known for speed. They might track Bel down but, by the time they did, she'd have been dead long enough to be nominated for sainthood.

If I can't get hold of a cop, I'm as good as sold.

Bel lifted her head. "Connell," she said, "how will we know when the Inn has been cleared?"

"Good question," said Morgan.

"I could nip around and take a peek," said Foy, still arrayed in his teeth and hair.

"Not a bad notion," said Morgan. "Look around, pick up some back-door gossip, see what's what."

"You might as well save time by taking a message when you go," said Bel. "If everything looks all right, you can deliver it. You'll know if it's all right, won't you, Ernie?"

Foy nodded.

"How does the plan sound to you, Connell?" Bel's face was a picture of uncertainty looking for reassurance. "Does it sound all right to you?"

Morgan nodded. "Exactly what I was going to suggest myself. We make a good team, my dear."

"What's the message, then?" Foy settled his teeth more comfortably and clacked them together.

"This is only if the Inn's been cleared," Morgan cautioned. "Be very sure you deliver this to the little secretary."

"It might not be Tetra," said Bel. "It might be Jinx, or somebody else from the ship." Security, most likely, or even Hessaphess, who knew?

"Somebody from the ship," said Morgan impatiently.

"Someone . . . appropriate," said Bel.

"I do understand," said Foy. "What's the message?"

Bel thought for a moment. "Tell them this is serious business. Tell them to find Freldt Saymak."

"Who?" Connell's lids narrowed his sapphire eyes to the merest chips.

"Someone authorized to handle this sort of thing," said Bel.

"Get the name right," said Morgan. "Freldt, is it? Freldt Saymak."

"I've got it, dear boy," Foy said, as he slipped out the door. "*You* aren't dealing with a fool."

Morgan fastened the door after the Wanderer. "Good riddance," he said. "The man is useful, but he lacks elegance."

He stood Bel up and lifted her again. "Now that we're alone. . . ," he began.

"Do you have such a thing as a bathroom around here?"

"I thought you went before you left the Inn."

Bel lifted her chin. "Well, really! Talk about lacking elegance!"

Morgan put Bel back on her feet. "I beg your pardon," he said. "You're quite right. Please pardon my crudity, my dear, but a man in my position, bereft of decent female company, may be forgiven for developing a certain roughness of manner, I hope. Er, it's this way."

"Aren't you going to untie me?"

"Is that really necessary?"

Bel forced a blush. "Well, really!"

"Sorry, my dear," said Connell, untying her. "No tricks, now. The front door is the only way out, and it's double-locked and barred. I seriously doubt you could overpower me, or distract me long enough to escape, don't you agree?"

Bel did.

She followed Morgan through the door opposite the exit. She had been afraid it might be a bedroom, and it might be more difficult to get back to the kitchen than it had been to leave it, but the room was empty. An open door revealed a storage closet, also empty. A closed door next to it probably concealed the same thing. Another closed door, Morgan opened, ushering Bel into a high-ceilinged water closet with a wave of his arm.

"Don't be long."

"I won't be rushed! I want to wash up while I'm in here. I feel grubby."

"Making yourself sweet and fresh?" Morgan's teeth gleamed.

"A lady always tries to look her best," said Bel.

"I'm afraid there's no mirror. No matter. You can always use my eyes, dear girl."

"For what?"

Connell laughed and bowed himself out.

Bel closed the door and locked it. "You aren't going to stand out there, are you? *That's* hardly necessary, is it?"

"I suppose not."

Bel listened to Morgan's oversized boots clumping away. She listened a moment longer, and heard them stealthily return to the door between the rooms.

Far enough away for her purpose.

First, she took care of business. She hadn't been kidding. Business concluded, she turned on the water in the rusty sink and checked things out.

The water closet had no window, worse luck. No pressurized cans, no razors, no bazookas. . . . No luck.

Bel sighed and washed up. She did feel grubby.

She came out damp, and smelling of cheap soap.

Morgan waited for her in the kitchen doorway but, instead of making a pass or passing a remark, he quickly bound her hands, then tied the end of the cord around the leg of the divan.

"I won't be a minute," he said.

As soon as he left the room, Bel sat on the floor, tilted the divan back with her shoulder, and slipped the cord down and off the leg.

What does he think I am — dumb, or something?

Knotted cords hold no terrors for a woman who's never had a jewelry organizer. Years of untangling necklace chains came to her aid now, as she worried the cord around her wrists with her teeth and the one around her ankles with her freed hands.

An unmistakable gurgle from the other room warned her to get some speed on.

She checked the door, on the off chance the big weasel had lied about the locks. She worked the bar easily, but the locks worked with keys, and Morgan had the keys.

Perhaps, when he came back, she could snuggle up to him and lift them.

No. The mind recoiled. The flesh crept.

Maybe a note, then.

Bel checked the windows. The one nearest the entrance had a hole in it the size of a walnut. She pulled at the board blocking the hole, and it gave; just barely, but just enough.

In the other room, water ran into the sink.

"Making himself sweet and fresh," Bel murmured. "Lord, have mercy."

Writing materials still cluttered the table. She scribbled a note, rolled it up, and poked it through the window.

Bel pushed the board back in place, and was sitting at the table when Morgan came in, also damp and smelling of cheap soap.

He gaped at Bel, and at the cord abandoned on the floor.

"I wanted to surprise you," Bel said. "I did, didn't I?"

~*~

Outside, the flounce-ridden female Wanderer kept her vigil. She berated herself for letting a tribesman slither past her on his way out. She had been tapping a rich vein of Urbanite guilt at the time, and the tribesman had been quick, but she'd have liked to winkle an update on upstairs events out of him.

She started as a roll of paper fell to the pavement nearby. She looked up, saw what might have been a slight movement at a boarded window, and picked up the paper.

She unrolled it. A message had been scrawled in Allesesperanto. "Get help! Prisoner Freldt Saymak Police Bel Schuster."

The Wanderer caught her breath, folded the note into a pellet and tucked it into the palm of her woolen mitt. She bent to pick up her bags when a hand gripped her shoulder.

The Stokk she'd last seen being followed away from this address by the District Criminal Investigator stood beside her. Another Stokk stood on her other side.

The one she'd seen before spoke. "Been here long?"

"A while," she said.

"Seen anybody go in or out?"

"Just an old Wanderer."

"In there now?"

"No."

The yellow Stokk released her.

"Move," said the other one.

Pron chided Ligniss with a subtle backhand to the mouth. "You could take a lesson from Korp Norstu," he said. "There she is, a bouncer, and a good one, but she never forgets what the Gunjin says about 'courtesy to our hosts.'"

"I was courteous," said Ligniss. "I didn't take her bags, did I?"

"Please forgive us," said Pron. He took some coins from his pocket and handed them to the woman. "Here's two bihts for you."

"Thank you, your honor. What's your favorite color?"

"I don't have a favorite color," said Pron. "Neither does Ligniss."

"I always liked red," said Ligniss. "Rusty, you know, like dried blood."

"Red, then," said Pron.

The woman hunted her flounces for ribbons of just the right shade, and tied them where she could to the Stokks' clothing.

"Many thanks," Pron said. Maybe he'd give this ribbon to Korp Norstu, when he got back to the Jipp Joint. Maybe she'd let him thread it through her left ear's grommets. The thought of it set him aflame.

"Thanks," said Ligniss.

The woman stepped aside to let them pass into the building. With a final scan of the streets for the DCI, she picked up her bags and took off at a trot.

~*~

In another part of the city, a report appeared on the desk of Communications Commissioner Darlla Bute. It showed an illegal transmission from the heart of mid-town. The transmission had been too brief to locate, but miscreants, she knew, seldom broke the law only once. When they repeated their infraction, she wanted to be ready for them.

"Assemble the team," said Bute. "We're going to make an example of these alley jammers."

The underling nodded and left the office.

Chapter 18

Ernie Foy, Jr. sidestepped the flouncy ribbon-peddler on the stoop. She was pulling a "talked out of my land by developers" routine on a middle-class Urbanite who'd never developed anything larger than his own paunch. The Urbanite blushed, though, and shuffled his feet, and Foy calculated the old woman was fishing in the rich waters of Urbanite Guilt. He silently wished her luck, and scrammed.

~*~

In an alley near Morgan's place, two hard-eyed children saw Foy go out and away, and conferred over it.

"Do we call in?" The girl spoke in an undertone, though no one was near enough to overhear.

"He's not a Stokk," said the boy. "Nor yet he's not a woman. Orders—"

"I know the orders," the girl said. "I was at Orgon's when the DCI called up, remember? I heard the descriptions the same time you did. That wasn't either one of them. It's activity, though."

"So's a tribeswoman selling ribbons," said the boy, who prided himself on his ability in comparative analysis. "You want to call it in?"

"No, but. . . ." Too late to follow the tribesman, anyway; he'd scuttled out of sight. "Waiting's no fun," the girl said.

The boy agreed. He hadn't wanted to come in the first place, but Orgon Peir had great force of personality, and the boy had taken the assignment in spite of himself.

"Might be some action later," the boy said, and they settled back down in hope.

~*~

Any child attempting to follow Foy would have been run off its little legs, assuming it wasn't lost in the maze of back streets and bolt-holes the Wanderer wriggled through.

Foy wasn't at all sure what he wanted to do, and skulking always helped him to think.

It might be safest to keep out of it, now. He could easily arrange to have been somewhere else all day; perhaps invisibility would be his wisest move. Foy didn't know much about Earthlings, but he knew Morgan, and he hadn't much hope of a fair deal from Bel's people if Morgan stood as an example.

On the other hand, he *could* be sure of a fair deal from the Llannonninn officers. He could forget about delivering Bel's message and turn Morgan in to the police.

And they'd go to Morgan's, and they'd find the kidnapped Union official, and she'd tell them about the message she'd told him to deliver, and everybody would want to know why he hadn't done it.

The Earthlings might even close ranks and stick him with the blame for the whole thing. If Morgan really did manage to force the Union to give him immunity, they'd have to hang his crimes on somebody. Foy had an idea those crimes would look awfully good on himself, especially if he disappeared at this critical moment.

Maybe it would be best, after all, to keep faith with the woman. Deliver her message, then go back to Morgan's and keep his hand in. If Morgan's deal went through, he'd be there to help shift the rap onto someone else and to collect his share of the ransom. If the wrath of the law descended, he could prove he'd been one of the good guys all along. If the whole thing went up in smoke, he'd give Morgan a token payment and take Bel into the country for a refreshing change of scam.

Foy removed an alley jammer from his pocket, where it had crawled, looking for crumbs, while the Wanderer had been lost in thought, and set his course for Jok'rel's.

~*~

Tetra straightened her tie and checked, once again, to reassure herself the credit voucher remained zipped securely in her money belt.

Captain Fazzaria had given her appearance an approving nod, and had handed over the voucher with confidence.

Tetra owed it to herself not to fail in her mission.

She wore, as the Captain had ordered, something soothing and apologetic, dignified, yet penitent: a black blouse and trousers, a black fitted tunic fastened along the left shoulder with silver starbursts, a silver sequined bow tie and a money belt of genuine black leather, with real metal zippers. It was a suit with class.

Knosh Jok'rel himself met her in the Inn's reception lounge. If he recognized her from the shore party, he gave no sign, but nodded curtly and led the way to his office.

~*~

District Criminal Investigator Pel Darzin stood at the bar, one booted foot on the brass rail. He had dismissed his squad, but stayed on, himself.

Jok'rel had lost considerable business when the officers cleared the bar. It was part of Darzin's job to apologize for the shortfall, and to offer him his choice of a krelp settlement or a tax deduction.

Jok'rel was occupied at the moment, though, and Darzin had decided to fill the time until their interview in questioning the staff.

It had been interesting, but not enlightening. Bookkeeper Freldt Saymak had played some cards with one of the Galactic Unionites. Shortly after Saymak had left the barroom, the leader of the Unionite party had ordered his people out with shocking bluntness.

Could the two events have been connected in some way? Darzin couldn't imagine how, but was it possible?

And why had the Unionite card player tarried when the

others had rushed out? And *was* she the Unionite card player? One of the waiters claimed it had been the Unionite who'd left early, and Freldt who'd lagged behind. *Had it been? And does it matter?*

Darzin shook his head and ordered a carbonated fruit drink.

~*~

Ernie Foy, Jr. watched the officers leave Jok'rel's Traveler's Rest Inn by twos and threes. Never one to take chances, he bypassed the main door, found a service entrance, and slunk in.

The whole ground floor was empty of customers. Even the taproom was still deserted, except for a man at the bar, dressed like a District Criminal Investigator. A smart guy like Foy knew that a man being dressed as a DCI didn't make him one. The covertness of this business with Morgan might require a certain amount of deception. Bel had said they would be working through unofficial channels. What better disguise could an unofficial non-native contact have, than the uniform of a native officer?

Foy was impressed.

He stepped up to the bar next to the supposed DCI and ordered a tube of local whiskey. "New here?"

"First time," said Darzin.

"You one of them?" Foy waved a hand at the scene of the shore party's disgrace.

Darzin, seeing the man gesture at the room from which he had just dismissed his Honor Squad, nodded.

"I have a message for you," said the man. "From Bel."

"Who's 'Bel'?"

Foy tapped his nose, nodded his head, and winked. "That's the ticket," he said. "The message is this: *'This is serious business. Find Freldt Saymak.'*"

"I don't have to find her," said Darzin. "I know where she is. Does she need help?"

"Now, I wouldn't know, would I?" Foy drained his whiskey tube and touched the brim of his hat, leaving it a tad greasier than before.

"Just a minute!" Darzin grasped his sleeve, only to have his fingers slip off. "Does this have to do with the Stokk Gord Pron? Is that what you meant by 'serious business'?"

"I just meant what I said. But I warn you as a friend," Foy said, thinking of Morgan when things didn't go his way, "the man can be dangerous when he's cornered."

"I believe you," said Darzin, who knew something about Stokk behavior. "But, what's your name, friend? You have a reward coming."

Foy laughed. "I'll get mine," he said. "Never fear me."

He lurked away.

Baffling, thought Darzin. That's what it was: Baffling.

None of the Irregulars had called yet to report any happening at Innkeeper Boktu Jippir's or at the house where the Stokk had left Bookkeeper Freldt Saymak.

Darzin had an uneasy feeling something *was* happening *somewhere*. Something hidden. Some unknown factor was showing its hand in the affair; to what purpose, Darzin couldn't have said.

Perhaps he should check on Freldt himself. See if the public-spirited Wanderer in the ribbons and flounces still kept watch. See if Orgon Peir had put the Irregulars in place as he'd promised. Just *see*.

Jok'rel's apology would have to wait. Darzin wrote a few words of regret on the back of his official card and left it with the substitute bartender.

"I'm expecting a call," Darzin told her. "Get a printout and hold it for me, will you? I'll check back later."

"Will do."

A bank of public modem booths filled one wall of the lobby, but anyone might come in, and Darzin couldn't risk being overheard by the wrong ears.

There was a public booth a couple of blocks away. Darzin ran into the street.

~*~

The visiphone behind the bar at Jok'rel's rang. The bartender switched on. The visual was blanked out, but a young voice said, "I'm calling for District Criminal Investigator Pel Darzin. He there?"

"He just left," said the barkeep. "He said to take a print."

"A print? Okay, but this might take some time."

The bartender polished her way down the bar but came back when the hesitant tapping stopped and the printer whirred.

"Be sure he gets it," the young voice said, and disconnected.

SUBJECT LEFT A. O AFTER, it said.

The bartender tore the paper off and stuck it under the bar. "Very important message," the bartender said, shaking her head with an indulgent smile. "Kids."

~*~

On his way to the public booth, Darzin came across two of his best officers listening to a twirlpiper and scanning the crowd for thieves.

"Officers Ander Patth and Ruah Maeek, come with me!"

The Officers fell in on either side of the Inspector.

~*~

The two hard-eyed children in the alley near Morgan's place perked up when they saw the Stokk approaching.

"That's him!" The girl elbowed the boy in the ribs. "Him and another one. And Orgon himself, right behind them."

The older boy slid into the alley where his subordinates waited.

"One of you go call the DCI," he said.

The girl bridled at the order. "Why don't *you* go call the DCI?"

"Because I'm the leader."

"Nobody ever asked for *my* vote!"

"That's because nobody cares," Orgon said, and the other boy laughed. "Now go call."

The girl waited until the Stokk went inside and the old woman they'd been talking to had trotted off. Then she darted out in search of a booth she could work for a free call. Had she waited, she would have seen the stooped and scrawny Wanderer she'd wanted to report on before creep up to the house from the other side. But she didn't.

She'd had a lot of luck with a phone a couple of blocks from Jok'rel's, so close she might as well save herself the trouble and report to Darzin in person.

Now, that's a funny thing. The old ribbon lady was in front of her, making excellent time in spite of her brimming sacks. As the girl watched, the woman ducked into an alley and stared across the street. The girl followed her stare, and saw the DCI himself, along with the well-known and popular Officers Patth and Maeek, hurrying toward surveillance point B.

When the three had passed, the woman left the alley and continued as she'd been going, now at a relaxed pace.

The girl considered following her, but decided to stick to the task she'd started and ran after Darzin.

~*~

District Criminal Investigator Pel Darzin was about half-way to surveillance point B when he heard the pattering of bare feet and felt a tug at his sleeve.

"Well, hello, there," said Officer Ruah Maeek, in her warm contralto. She was very good at singing tragic ballads, was Officer Ruah Maeek.

A hard-eyed child waved a grubby hand at the officers, but spoke to Darzin, whom she had met at the library when he was a mere patrolman and she a mere hard-eyed tot.

"Juvenile Genesis Selinsky, of the Irregulars," she identified herself. "That Stokk is at the old house. Him and another one. They just got there a minute or two ago."

"Two of them! What did the other one look like?"

"Sort of light orange. Blue hair. No lips. You know, like a Stokk."

It wasn't Innkeeper Boktu Jippir, himself, then. *Too bad.*

"Sounds like Stokk Utrop Ligniss," said Officer Ander Patth, who always read the circulars. "Strongarm man for Innkeeper Boktu Jipper."

Close enough for twirlpipe music, thought Darzin.

Chapter 19

"I wanted to surprise you," said Bel. "I did, didn't I?"

"You did, indeed," said Connell Morgan. "If you don't mind, my dear. . . . Exactly how. . . ?"

"Ahh," said Bel. "That would be telling. You don't plan to tie me up again, do you, Connell?"

"Not unless you want me to, my dear."

Bel did a stress-management exercise to combat nausea and said, "Some other time, perhaps."

Bel saw Morgan scanning the room to see what else she might have accomplished. He passed over the door, then came back to it. He shook his head, split a calculating glance between Bel and the cords on the floor, and looked at the door again.

What does he think? I jimmied the locks? Where does he think I've been hiding the crowbar?

Too bad she hadn't been able to. Then Bel decided to try a trick so simple, so puerile, so clankingly unsophisticated, she could only credit her long association with young people for her having thought of it. She decided to tell a truth.

"I couldn't get the locks undone," she said. "As you see, I left the door bolted, too; if I couldn't undo the locks, there didn't seem to be much point in taking off the bolt."

"Well," said Connell, as many another wise and indulgent adult might have done in his place, "we'll just leave the bolt on, then. As for the locks. . . ."

He took the keys from his pocket.

Bel, unable to resist pressing her luck, said, "You mean you're going to let me out?"

"Very nice try, my dear," said Connell. One after the other, with what he meant to be crushing deliberateness, he put the keys in the locks and turned them. He fiddled a bit doing it, grumbling that he could never remember which way the blasted things turned. He crossed to between Bel and the divan and took her hand, attempting, unsuccessfully, to draw her from her seat at the table. "As I say, I am surprised. Agreeably so. I like a woman who — Now what?"

Quiet but heavy footsteps ascended the stairs and stopped outside the door. Connell motioned Bel to silence.

The person or persons unknown stood mute outside the door for the space of ten standard Earthling heartbeats. Then a voice said, very quietly, "Freldt Saymak."

Bel felt suddenly lightheaded. Foy had gotten through! Or Freldt had been on hand when Bel's disappearance had first been noted. "Yes!"

"No," Morgan growled softly. "I want my guarantees before I deal in person." In a voice as harsh as his honeyed tones could sound, he said, "Be off with you! Out you are and out you'll stay, until I have what I want!"

The door handle turned, the door pressed against the bar. "Off, I tell you!"

Bel's giddiness passed. "I'm coming!" She launched from her chair and threw back the bolt.

"But I locked—" said Connell. He stopped as the door swung wide, and two Stokk stepped in, closing the door behind them. One was yellow, with Kelly green hair. The other was apricot, his hair a bronze blue. Each wore a rusty red ribbon, just the color of dried blood.

~*~

Foy left Jok'rel's with the satisfying feeling that his duty had been done. In fact, he felt so secure he took the second most direct route back to Morgan's, arriving at a good peeking point in time to see a pair of Stokk approach the hovel.

They stopped, and that pest of a bag lady fell into conversation with them.

She had nerve, Foy certainly gave her credit. Very few people cared to hit the Stokk up for change, as the Stokk had a tendency to hit back. But the old Wanderer did it, and succeeded, by the look of it.

Foy watched in awe as they allowed the tribeswoman to tie ribbons onto their clothing, and in perplexity as they entered Morgan's hideout.

What could a pair of Stokk want with Morgan? The contact had asked about a Stokk. Stokk Gord Pron. Could one of these be Stokk Gord Pron? And, again, what could a Stokk want with Morgan? What could a Stokk have to do with a visiting Galactic Union dignitary?

Maybe the old tribeswoman could give him a clue. She had spoken to them, after all. Maybe they had dropped a word he could turn to account.

The old woman foiled him by picking up her bags and trotting away down the street.

A grubby girl popped out of an alley and fell in behind the elderly female Wanderer.

The old woman had better look sharp. She won't keep her takings long if that child gets close enough to cut a hole in those bags.

Foy waited another moment to see if anyone else came out of the woodwork, then, cautiously, he crept up to the door. He listened, but heard nothing. In utter silence, not even daring to breathe, the old man eased open the door, and heard the name, "Freldt Saymak."

The door at the top of the stairs opened, and the Stokk entered.

Foy crept up the steps, pressed against the wall to avoid creaking treads.

~*~

Bel and Morgan both recognized the yellow Stokk with the green hair. Both had seen him at the Inn: Bel remembered how he had followed her out, attempting to speak to her; Morgan remembered how he had gotten in the way until the twirlpiper's crowd had given Morgan the advantage. Both remembered his interruption of Morgan's move in the alley.

Both Earthlings assumed, with reluctance, the Stokk must be working with the Llannonninn police. It seemed unlikely to the point of impossibility, but here they were, saying what amounted to a password, and one of them had been around from Bel's first misstep. Nothing but an official police involvement could account for it, unless one posited a separate set of circumstances that just happened to fit, like a piece from a jigsaw puzzle shaped exactly like the missing piece of another.

Neither Earthling wondered, by now, at the ribbons.

"I told you this is none of your business," said Morgan.

"So you did," said Pron. The two Earthlings had apparently been having quite a time. They were both damp, and smelled of cheap soap; they had evidently called a truce long enough to wash off the blood and dirt.

Pron congratulated himself on his timing. During a truce, couples always became much easier to deal with. Statistics showed more hovercraft sales were made during truces than at any other time of the mating cycle.

While Ligniss threw the bolt and positioned himself in front of the door, Pron spoke to "Saymak."

"No introduction?"

Bel shook her head.

The first Stokk spoke to the man. "Gord Pron," he said, indicating himself. "My friend, here, is Utrop Ligniss. We don't want any trouble—"

Ligniss failed to suppress a laugh.

Pron had to smile a bit, himself. "Well," he amended, "we're willing to do without it, if that'll get us the quickest, most satisfactory arrangement."

Morgan relaxed. This was more like it. No trouble. Quick and satisfactory arrangement. Just what he wanted, himself.

"Here are my terms," he said.

"Shut up," said Gord Pron. "I'm talking to the lady."

"Now, just a minute," said Morgan, who felt, not without reason, he was losing the upper hand.

"About my friend Ligniss," Pron said to Morgan. "Don't get the idea he wears those baggy clothes because he doesn't know how to dress. It's the muscles. They get used a lot. They flex. He kept ripping out the seams of his regular clothes, and elastic makes him cranky."

Ligniss nodded, his narrow gray eyes twinkling his delight at being the subject of conversation.

"Ligniss is very high-strung," said Pron. "Show them your hands, Ligniss."

The apricot Stokk raised his fists. They weren't overly large, but they seemed to be constructed of some material that could withstand the test of time.

"Notice the knuckles," said Pron. "How sharply knobby they are. He cracks them, you see. Against parts of other people's bodies."

Morgan sank onto the divan. "Poor fellow," he said. "They don't hurt you, I hope? No aching, no feeling of weakness in the joints?"

Ligniss shook his head and lowered his weapons.

Pron turned back to Bel. "I like the way you operate," he said. "The way you slipped away from the DCI and his bunch."

Bel snickered. *The Deesy Eye.* She didn't know what 'Deesy' meant but, from the way Pron said it, she bet it wasn't complimentary to poor old Hessaphess. "I didn't exactly do it on purpose," she had to admit. "I only planned to go as far as the lobby door."

Gord Pron said, "But that just wasn't good enough, was it?"

"No," said Bel. "It wasn't." By golly, these people were

more understanding than an off-limits professor had any right to expect.

"Then *this* one showed up," Pron said, with a wave toward Morgan, "and wouldn't be denied."

"Wait till I tell you," said Bel. "He thinks—"

"I'm a man," said Pron. "I know what he thinks. I can't say I blame him, having seen you fight."

Wait a minute. Bel got the feeling of having one's brain tweaked that comes when one first suspects one is dreaming.

"You'd be a worthy opponent, Freldt Saymak," said Pron. "I'm almost sorry you didn't try to work against me with the police."

~*~

Foy waited to hear no more.

Slipped away from the DCI, eh? Didn't try to work against the Stokk with the police, eh? And the contact had asked about this very Gord Pron. And Freldt Saymak was apparently in there, as well, had probably arrived in Foy's absence, and the contact had said he knew where she is, which proved . . . something.

No wonder Bel Schuster wanted to avoid official channels. Well, Foy would just see about that. After all, he might be a sneak and a thief, a fraud and a double-crossing me-firster, but he hoped he was always a good citizen. Besides, if the Stokk had their thumbs in the pie, it was a foregone conclusion who would end up full of juice and who would be left holding the empty pan.

He slunk back down the steps and went looking for an officer. He had to find the real DCI, and he figured he had to find him fast.

~*~

"Um," said Bel.

"But she isn't—" said Morgan.

"Connell," Bel said, "the man told you to shut up."

"Exactly so," said Pron. "Maybe he's hard of hearing, Ligniss. Maybe you'd better stand closer to him. Then, if we have to tell him again, we'll be sure he listens."

Ligniss sat down beside Morgan and Pron took his place in front of the door.

"So, Bookkeeper Freldt Saymak," Pron said. "Are you prepared to give me your answer?"

Bel wasn't blessed with one of those memories which could replay conversations verbatim, but it's amazing what a common intelligence can do with two million volts of adrenaline plugged into it. Now she remembered how eager Bookkeeper Freldt Saymak had been to switch clothes and places at the table with her. She remembered how Freldt had been the first to notice their switch had fooled Wotan Hessaphess. "Even him," Bel remembered the bookkeeper saying. "We fooled *even him.*" The implication, Bel now saw, was obvious. If they had fooled a Space Trooper, assigned to keep his deesy eye firmly fixed on the personnel, they had certainly fooled *Someone Else.* Someone, for example, such as a Stokk who wanted an answer involving something in which the police would be interested.

Bel cleared her throat. "Would you repeat the question?"

~*~

Not too far off, a be-flounced and be-ribboned old female Wanderer hauled her bags through the door of a disreputable-looking dive. Anyone arriving a scant moment later would have seen no sign of her.

Chapter 20

What's Bookkeeper Freldt Saymak up to? The DCI thought he had made it clear she wasn't to risk injury or worse. When she had found herself, for whatever reason, unable to wait for Darzin or his agent at the Inn, she should have agreed to anything and let Darzin handle it from there.

Perhaps he hadn't made it clear. Perhaps Bookkeeper Freldt Saymak had tried to evade the Stokk until Darzin's arrival. Perhaps that's why she had left the Inn, meaning to return when she knew the Stokk's proposal could be overheard.

And the Stokk had struck. He had herded her away from safety, taken her prisoner, left her alone in fear, and returned with this Strongarm Man Utrop Ligniss to force her into the Stokk web of evil.

Not bad at all. Because she would agree. The Stokk would release her, and she would bring charges for abduction and intimidation. Darzin would have the Stokk and, with them, a crack to pry at to get to the Grand Councilor behind them.

But, then, what did her message mean? What serious business was this mysterious "Bel" warning him about? And why did the man in the greasy hat call Pron a dangerous man when he was cornered? Pron wouldn't be acting so openly if he had any suspicion of being observed. And nobody wanted to corner him; they wanted to let him walk away from his "extortion victim" and then hit him with a summons.

Everything about this case was simple and clear but that message… unless this "Bel" knew everything. It all made sense if Bel knew about the Grand Councilor, the Stokk, Bookkeeper Freldt Saymak's call to Darzin, the bookkeeper's abduction by the Stokk, Darzin's plan to prosecute the Stokk for the abduction, *and knew that the Stokk knew Darzin's plan, too.*

Yes, now all of it made sense. Of course the Stokk realized he could be prosecuted for abduction. He had acted rashly, and Innkeeper Boktu Jippir had sent him scurrying back to where he'd stashed his victim. Soon, the station house would get a call for DCI Pel Darzin. It would be Stokk Gord Pron, offering to trade the bookkeeper's life for Darzin's silence.

Darzin's first priority was to get access to a phone, an official one, and one that wouldn't tie him down.

"Officer Ander Patth, I need a mobile modem. I'll wait for it here, then we'll go on. A call may be coming through for me at any moment. I want it soonest."

The officer sprinted away.

~*~

"Why do you want me to repeat it?" Gord Pron smirked. "You want a witness? I have a witness, too."

Utrop Ligniss waved a knotty hand.

"Our word against yours," said Pron. "Two against one usually carries the weight in court."

"But there's two of *us*," said Bel.

"There won't be, if it comes to court," said Pron.

"Of course," said Bel. "Silly of me."

Morgan closed his eyes and clasped his hands. "Hail Mary, quite contrary. . . ." He looked at Bel in confusion. "That isn't right, is it?"

Bel spoke to the Stokk. "I want to be sure I don't make any mistakes. I don't believe you're a man who would tolerate mistakes."

"Smart," said Pron. "Didn't I always say you're smart? Here it is, then, without the sucrose coating. Cook Jok'rel's books so business looks worse than it is. *Make* the business worse than it is. Deposit receipts in your own account, and lose the paper on them. You can keep anything you embezzle; all we want is the Inn."

Yes, the police would probably find all this most interesting. One wondered why Saymak hadn't risked telling them about it, rather than putting a total stranger in the soup.

But, of course, telling the police is exactly what Freldt Saymak did! Gord Pron had been breathing on her, pressing her for an answer. She had to sidetrack him long enough to contact the police. So, she had snookered Bel into switching places with her. Bel and her group were confined to the Inn; it hadn't occurred to the desperate bookkeeper the decoy would light out for parts unknown.

The police must be looking for her even now. They had been alerted to Pron's criminal interest in "her" as soon as Freldt Saymak reached for a phone.

It explained why the shore party had pulled out: to clear the decks for the local law. And it explained why the officers were all over the Inn: All that moonshine about an insult to the Innkeeper and calling in the Ambassador was just a cover for the police activity.

Bel heartily wished she had stayed in the Inn, as she'd been told. None of this would have happened. She resigned herself to (under the circumstances, she eagerly yearned for) the stiffest penalty the law allowed.

On the other hand, the law seemed to be looking for Morgan, as well as Pron. If they found one, they would find the other, and she had managed to get a coded message to Tetra Petrie.

It might count for something. It *would* count for something, if Bel got a chance to speak.

In the meantime, help converged from every quarter. Officers, Councilors, perhaps even the incendiary Harry Chestney, all of these, with the efficiency which comes from coordinated speed, must be straining every resource to locate her. Once they did, they would storm the place, form a defensive ring around the innocent civilian, and carry the criminals off in chains.

Bel liked it.

All she had to do was stall, keep the Stokk occupied and on the spot, for just a short while longer.

~*~

Officer Ander Patth loped back to where he had left District Criminal Investigator Pel Darzin. An old Wandering Tribesman in a greasy hat reached out a hand to stop him, but he waved the man toward another officer and ran on.

The mobile modem clumped against his side, heavy in its padded case.

Officer Ander Patth lived for adventure. It was why he had gone into police work. So far, he hadn't experienced much in the way of real adventure, the colorful stuff of which best-selling autobiographies are made. This looked to be different.

Chapter One, Officer Ander Patth said to himself, saving his breath for locomotion, *The Early Years. Chapter Two, I Enter the Force. Chapter Three. . . . Chapter Three. . . .* The subtitle of Chapter Three would have to wait until he had some idea of what was going on here. He had no doubt, though, of his own centrality to the outcome.

"Your modem, Sir," he said, halting by Pel Darzin and snapping a smart salute. He held the case while Darzin opened it and extracted the unit.

Darzin put the headpiece on first: It was simply an elastic headband and two curved metal strips. One strip positioned a small viewscreen three inches away and towards the outside corner of one's eye. The other band gently pressed an earphone to one's ear and continued, to hold a microphone near one's mouth. The other part of the unit was a glove with a keypad on the back of the hand. There was also a mini-printport one could clip to one's belt. Darzin did so.

While the DCI put on his gear, Patth reported.

"I took the liberty of asking if any calls had come for you at the station house. None had."

"You didn't ask specifically about a call from a Stokk, did you? Or mention Stokk at all?"

"No, Sir! I asked about any calls in general and signed the unit out in my name. Said I was doing crowd control over by Jok'rel's and thought I might need it."

"Good man," said Darzin.

Chapter Three, thought Officer Ander Patth. *I Prove My Mettle.*

~*~

Connell Morgan crushed down his panic and tried to straighten out his facts. He had snatched a Galactic Union dignitary. The Stokk who had kept getting in the way had been after the same woman, under the mistaken impression the dignitary was a Llannonninn bookkeeper. Easy to see how it had happened: the clothes switch, which had been so obvious to Morgan, had not been obvious to the Stokk, to whom most Earthlings looked alike.

A natural mistake, and one easily cleared up.

"Excuse me," Morgan said.

Ligniss cracked his knuckles.

Morgan rubbed the dent on the side of his head.

"You still seem to be having trouble making up your mind," Pron said to Bel. "Maybe I'd better help you."

"It isn't that," said Bel. "I'm just thinking about how to do it. Juggling books isn't something you can just r'ar back and do. It takes planning, and groundwork. It takes time."

Pron shook his head. "You walk out of here, you go to your office, and you start fiddling the files. If you can't siphon off some krelps for yourself along the way, it's your hard luck. All I care about is making Jok'rel feel glad he's got a pal who'll take a losing business off his hands. See?"

"I see. I also see Jok'rel's 'pal' taking over the losing business and discovering some nasty person has been fiddling the files. I see a trip to the country for a bookkeeper of our mutual acquaintance."

Pron lounged against the door and exchanged an appreciative glance with Utrop Ligniss.

"I'll tell you what," Pron said to Bel. "We'll trade paper on it. I have a contract here." He pulled one from an inside pocket of his flashy suit. "I filled in what we want from you before I came. I wasn't planning on filling in what you get out of it. You weren't going to get anything out of it except your health and whatever you could skim. But you've made me change my mind. I'm going to promise you immunity from prosecution. After Jok'rel's isn't Jok'rel's anymore, you can come in and quietly put things right. We can trust you to do it for the same reason we trust our Stokk bookkeepers." He paused for effect, and said one word: "Auditors."

A chill ran up Bel's spine. "Alligators," he might have said. "Ambulances."

"You can trust me, all right," she said. "But how can I trust you? Okay, so maybe you can promise not to prosecute. Maybe you'll even keep your promise. But what about Jok'rel? What about the Galactic Union? Jok'rel's and the GU have a contract, don't they? The GU has a way of looking into things like sudden turnovers of facilities they do business with."

Pron laughed. "Let them look," he said. "They won't see anything except what we want them to see."

"How do you plan to arrange that?"

"Suppose I told you," said Pron, "we have a friend on the Grand Council."

Hot dog! This would be the card to take the trick, assuming she lived to play out her hand. "A friend on the Grand Council? I'd say I don't believe it."

"It's true."

"Who?"

"Never mind who."

"Well, I don't believe it, then. And I'm not going to sign anything."

Pron tossed the contract onto the table.

Bel came to her feet, her chair skidding across the floor and back against the wall. It just seemed like a good time not to be caught with one's moving gear folded up under a table.

At a signal from Pron, Utrop Ligniss jerked Morgan to his feet and into a full nelson.

Morgan gave an incoherent cry.

"Stop it!" Bel might relish the thought of Connell Morgan being carted away in handcuffs, but she shrank from his having his head popped like a cork.

"Gently, Ligniss," said Pron. "We're still negotiating."

"I think I can crack him just enough to give him a permanent headache," said Ligniss. "I've been wanting to try it out, see if I've got the leverage and pressure right. Can I?"

"No!" Morgan wiggled ineffectually. "Say 'No'!"

Bel decided she'd stalled long enough. She unfolded the contract.

"You wanted to fill something in."

"Sorry," said Pron. "You missed your chance."

Bel signed the bookkeeper's name and pushed the contract back across the table. So, the Stokk thought he had Freldt's signature on an incriminating document, and he didn't. *Too bad.*

"Let him go," Pron said.

Ligniss released Morgan and helped him straighten his disarranged clothing.

"Now," Pron said to Bel, tucking the contract into his suit. "I'm going to escort you back to the Inn. Ligniss will stay here with your boyfriend. Thinking about what he might do to those pretty white teeth will encourage you to hurry."

Chapter 21

Council City Communications Commission Official Darlla Bute thought of herself as a beklemek. If she had been Earthling, she would have thought of herself as a spider but, being Llannonninn, a beklemek was the appropriate creature for comparison.

ComCom Official Darlla Bute didn't *look* like a beklemek. Darlla Bute had large, wide-set topaz eyes and short red hair with a fringe of bangs. A beklemek, on the other hand . . . well, a beklemek didn't look anything like that. But it was patient; that's the point.

ComCom Official Darlla Bute and her BLITS (Block and Locate Illegal Transmitter Signals) Team cruised the midtown area in their specially equipped hovervan. As they cruised, Darlla Bute studied a bank of monitors.

One of the monitors showed a map of the midtown area, with the buildings which hadn't requested or been granted transmitter licenses, yet had transmitted, in defiance of the law, picked out in red. The van's position, indicated by a green rectangle, showed Official Darlla Bute her position relative to the unlicensed locations.

Four other monitors showed the street fore and aft and to either side of the vehicle.

A fifth screen filled with data which the Search-and-Seize program pulled and displayed as the van passed one of the red-code buildings.

The sixth screen was blank. It would show what went on inside, should the BLITS Team enter a target. Official Darlla Bute planned on having someone else monitor the sixth screen when the time came. She planned on being one of the figures *on* the screen.

As for now, Council City Communications Commission Official Darlla Bute was content to wait and scan.

Just like a beklemek.

~*~

Council City's midtown section wasn't large. It was, perhaps, inevitable that Official Darlla Bute's patrol would cross the path of DCI Pel Darzin.

Inevitable or not, it happened.

In the ordinary run of things, the BLITS team and the DCI's squad would have waved to each other and gone their separate ways, but Darzin wore a mobile communications unit. Although the unit was small, to Darlla Bute's trained eye it stuck out like a pratty in a chorus line.

Interesting. . . . The ComCom Official punched up a screen of data on mobile unit dispensations. None had been signed out to DCI Pel Darzin. There had been one issued, though, to Officer Ander Patth, one of Darzin's best and brightest.

"Stop the van," Bute said. "Park it."

The ComCom agent at the steering stick pulled up to an empty parking space and sidled into it.

Bute got out and waited for Darzin and his crew to come up to her.

~*~

Darzin had a pretty good idea what she wanted, and he cursed his luck. ComCom Officials were notoriously hardnosed. In fact, it was a common wheeze around the squadroom that the Galactic Union wanted free trade with Llannonn in order to acquire ComCom Official noses for industrial use.

The DCI could only hope this Official would prove to be more reasonable than most.

"We have a discrepancy in our records," said Bute.

Darzin felt his stomach clench, though he gave no outward sign. *I knew it.*

"*Chapter Four*," muttered Officer Ander Patth, "*A Blighted Career.*"

"We show Officer Ander Patth requested a unit for use in crowd control. I don't see Officer Patth controlling a crowd or wearing a unit, but I do see a unit on you, while our records fail to reflect the issuance of a unit in your name. Would you care to help us correct this error?"

"Communications Commission Official Darlla Bute," said Darzin, "none of us believe you think there's an error in your records. I appreciate your graciousness, but ComCom records are legendary in their accuracy."

This, as Darzin knew, was a certain path to Darlla Bute's good side.

"Then, District Criminal Investigator Pel Darzin," said Bute, her attitude of formal hostility cranked down by several notches, "would you mind telling me what's going on?"

"Communications Commission Official Darlla Bute," said the DCI, "I'm going to have to ask you to trust me. I have a reason for what I'm doing, even a reason for why I'm concealing it. Please believe my cause is just."

"Your cause may be just," said Bute, "but your unit is in somebody else's name. I'm sorry to be so insistent, but I must have an explanation."

Darzin hesitated but a moment. He wanted very much to trap the renegade Councilor. He felt his chances decrease with every additional person who knew about this sting, but his chances would diminish to zero if Officer Bute pulled him in on a ComCom charge.

"Very well," he said, and he told her.

"Could he already have made the ransom call you expect? Earlier?"

"How much earlier?"

Bute told him the time of the call which had galvanized her Team to action.

Darzin shook his head. "He wasn't there, then."

"But," said Bute, "if there's an illegal transmitter in there, someone else could have used it. Someone left to guard this Bookkeeper. The Bookkeeper herself."

"If she did," said Darzin, "it would have been purely as a way of drawing attention to herself. She didn't know I saw her taken, or that I was able to follow the Stokk to his lair. She must be desperate."

"Tell it to the judge," said Darlla Bute. "Meanwhile, I think we have probable cause. I think we'll just hit this place." She signaled her hovervan to slide into the traffic stream. "Lead the way, District Criminal Investigator Pel Darzin."

"No!"

"No?"

"You're within your authority," said Darzin, grinding out an ingratiating smile, "but I beg you, no. You see, there's more to this than I've told you yet. A Grand Councilor is in this. In it on the wrong side. I'm certain one of the Grand Council is working with the Stokk. I don't know who or why, but I'm certain of it. If I can get this Stokk under arrest without attracting undue attention. . . ."

"You might also get your proof. I understand."

"So, you see, that's why Officer Ander Patth requested the communications unit in his name under false pretenses."

Meanwhile, Officer Ruah Maeek had been in conference with the child.

"District Criminal Investigator Pel Darzin," said the contralto, "the child has additional information. About activity in and around the subject house."

"Yes, Juvenile Genesis Selinsky," said Darzin. "What more can you tell us?"

The grubby little girl told of the old ribbon lady's presence on the stoop, of her race away when the Stokk had entered the house, and of her sudden lack of urgency when the DCI had passed.

Darzin nodded in satisfaction. The good citizen had, indeed, kept faith. She had been rushing to report the Stokk's return when she had seen the DCI and had correctly assumed he was already on his way back to the house.

Then, with an air of vindication, the girl told of the old Wandering Tribesman who had left some time before the Stokk had arrived.

"Describe him," said Darzin, his vanilla wafer skin paling to sugar cookie.

The girl described the tribesman, with a wealth of detail and an unbecoming sneer for her fellow Irregular.

Darzin gasped. "The man with the message!"

"What message?" Bute's attitude developed a touch of frost. "So you *did* receive an illegal transmission!"

"He delivered the message in person," said Darzin, rather stiffly. "It had nothing to do with transmissions." *Or did it?* Had the man with the message been the one who'd made the illegal transmission the ComCom Official was so wired about? If he had, who had he called?

Everything fell into place like a squad scrambling into formation. Of course the old Tribesman had made the illegal transmission. And he had called . . . the mysterious Bel! She had told him to get out of it and warn the DCI.

Darzin addressed the child. "Did this Tribesman come back to the house?"

"Not that I saw. Orgon Peir and Abnaki Segayk were watching when I left; you could ask them."

Darzin turned again to Darlla Bute. "You see how it is," he said. "This Tribesman is probably your guilty party, and he's gone."

"Possibly," Darlla Bute conceded. "Although he might have returned by now."

"And then there's Bel," said Darzin.

"Who's Bel?"

"Ah," said Darzin. "Who, indeed? She sent the message the Tribesman brought me; a warning to find Freldt Saymak, a warning that Pron is dangerous when cornered, a warning that this is 'serious business.'"

"Serious is right," said Bute. "If this Bel person has placed or accepted an illegal transmission—"

"Then 'this Bel person' has done so in the service of Llannonn," said Darzin. "Let's get our priorities straight, ComCom Official Darlla Bute."

"I have nothing but your unsubstantiated word for any of this, District Criminal Investigator Pel Darzin," said Bute. When Darzin had finished gnashing his teeth, she continued, "Nevertheless, I'm inclined to believe you. I suggest we proceed to this unlicensed house and question the people this child says have been on watch there."

"Agreed."

Darzin led the way.

Juvenile Genesis Selinsky enraged her Irregular companions by pointedly refraining from crowing over the DCI's interest in a character one of them, at least, had mocked her for noticing. It was a grand day for Juvenile Genesis Selinsky.

"Yeah, he come back," Juvenile Abnaki Segayk told Darzin, vindictively adding, "just after *she* left. If she'd turned around, she could've spit on him. He went in for a minute, then come out and run off again."

"After the Stokk went up?"

"Yeah."

"Did he see the Stokk go in?"

"Dunno. But he come out faster than he went in."

"I wonder. . . ," said Darzin. "Now what. . . . I wish I could lay hands on that Tribesman."

"Shall I fetch him for you?" Officer Ruah Maeek was happy to offer.

"Do you know where he is?"

"Over there," she said, while Officer Ander Patth did some tooth-gnashing of his own. "At least, a man answering to his description is lurking in that alley, with a mysterious woman in black."

Chapter 22

Tetra Petrie rose and hooked thumbs with Knosh Jok'rel in the traditional Llannonninn sign of good faith.

"I don't think I could have asked for more," the Innkeeper said. "I'd like to know why your people left in the first place, and why you don't know whether or not you'll come back, but I understand about it being top-secret. I knew there'd be weird problems come up when I signed a contract with aliens. No offense, I hope."

"No offense," said Tetra. "And thank you for the pamphlets." She patted her bulging belt-bag, packed with brochures entitled LLANNONNINN ETIQUETTE – DO'S AND DON'T'S FOR OUR OFFWORLD GUESTS.

"It still beats me why you weren't sent some of these before."

"Some foul-up in administration," Tetra said. "Sector Command will probably send us more copies than we have people after we have left orbit."

"I hear you talking," said Jok'rel. "Well, listen, I just want to run these figures through the program, set the credits up in a holding account. Are you in a hurry to get back to the ship?"

"No, not particularly."

"Go on into the bar, then." Jok'rel handed Tetra a slip of paper the size of a theater ticket. "Give this to the ven on duty in there; it's good for as much of anything as you want. I'll have you transferred back up as soon as I get this squared away."

"Fine," said Tetra. "Thank you."

The assignment had not been difficult. Jok'rel had been more hurt than enraged, and had been delighted when Tetra had offered the hand and credit voucher of peace. Tetra's paternal grandmother had given her good advice when she'd told her that *please, thank you, I'm sorry* and *you're welcome* were magic words. *Here's some money* were good ones, too.

Tetra gave the bartender her ticket and ordered a ladylike glass of sherry.

~*~

Near the Bird on a Barseat, a disreputable-looking dive in the heart of midtown, Ernie Foy, Jr. tried to flag down an officer already headed in the proper direction. Ander Patth (for it was he) waved the Tribesman toward another member of the Force.

Just as well. This is too big to waste on an officer. I'll take this to the top. Of course, the top would be the Grand Council. He wasn't quite prepared to put himself in the way of the Grand Council. *I'll take this to the middle-management level.*

"Excuse me," said Foy to the indicated Officer, "I'm looking for the District Criminal Investigator."

"District Criminal Investigator Pel Darzin was at Jok'rel's when I left there. May still be there, may be gone. If he's gone, probably be somebody there who can tell you where."

Foy thanked him and scuttled back to the Inn. He hadn't seen anybody but the disguised Galactic Union agent when he'd been at Jok'rel's before but, naturally, the DCI had been in the Innkeeper's office, apologizing for the inconvenience.

This time, Foy came on official business; he used the front door with the flamboyant piety of a backslider on Easter Sunday.

The barroom had been lucky for him before.

Sure enough, someone was in there; a woman in a black uniform with a row of starbursts across one shoulder.

Must be a Regional Investigative Coordinator at the very least. That must've been some inconvenience.

The possible RIC sat at a table. Unless she was kneeling on the floor, she was the shortest adult Foy had ever seen in a uniform. *The little 'uns are the worst.* He congratulated himself heartily for being an informer, rather than an informed-upon.

"You again?" The bartender's greeting was not a jolly one, for Foy had melted away before without paying.

"Forgot something," said Foy, pushing six bihts across the counter with a sickly grin.

The bartender took the coins gingerly and carried them into a pool of good light to check their numbers against a list supplied by the local police.

Foy fidgeted, eying the supposed RIC. Now that the moment was upon him, he shrank from it. Maybe he could just drop a hint and leave. Do his duty without getting involved. If worse came to worst, and Morgan or Bel tried to throw some of their guilt off onto him, the RIC could testify in his behalf. *Yes. Okay.*

Tetra saw Foy enter with fascinated distaste. She had never seen so many sorts of uncleanliness concentrated in so limited a space before, and ambulatory, to boot.

And then he sat down at her table.

"DCI Pel Darzin gone, then?"

"I could not say," said Tetra, trying in vain to catch the barkeep's eye.

Foy tapped nervously at the table, then rubbed the fingerprints off with a grimy sleeve. *She's playing it cagey. Bad sign.* Whenever the Force started losing transparency, somebody was in big trouble. Foy didn't want that somebody to be himself. Maybe a higher degree of cooperation than he'd previously contemplated wouldn't be out of order.

"You're his superior," Foy said, and waited for assent.

Tetra shared a family trait of considering herself superior to most people. Part of her superiority, however, involved the illusion that she never let anyone know she felt superior. Tetra was short, but she was never small.

"I could not say," she repeated.

"I have information," Foy said, tossing his discretion and not caring where it landed. "About a crime in progress."

"You want to inform the police, do you not?"

Foy clasped his hands together so hard they shook. "Oh, yes," he said. "Yes, I do." He leaned across the table. "It started out as a simple kidnapping for ransom. The victim was a Galactic Union official named Bel Schuster. At least, that's what I was told. I didn't do it, you understand, I only know who did."

"Bel Schuster!"

"You know the name. Have they got you on the case?"

"I could not say."

"Oh, my. All right. But be careful; there's something more to it. This Bel Schuster sent me here earlier with a message: Find Freldt Saymak."

"You delivered the message?"

"Yes."

"To whom?"

"To the Galactic Union agent. He said he knew where Freldt Saymak is and asked me about—"

"What Galactic Union agent?"

"The one disguised as a District Criminal Investigator." A terrible suspicion struck Foy to the heart, but Tetra was too quick for him.

"Oh, *that* Galactic Union agent," she said. "Excellent. Go on. What did he ask you about?"

"He asked me about the Stokk Gord Pron. If he's involved."

"Yes, I know about the Stokk Gord Pron." That was the Stokk Freldt had told them about. *Freldt.* . . . "The agent said he knew where Freldt Saymak is?"

"Yes," said Foy. "He asked me if she's in danger."

"How would *you* know?"

"That's what *I* said. Then I found out. I left the agent here and went back to . . . to where Bel Schuster is. I saw two Stokk going in. I followed, and listened at the door. One of them called himself Gord Pron, and he was talking to Freldt Saymak! He spoke to her by name. So, you see, the Galactic Union's in this, whatever it is."

Tetra was glad someone else seemed to be as much at a loss as she was. *Whatever it is, is right.* "I take it the Stokk is not the original kidnapper?"

"No, of course not. Do I look like a man who would work with a Stokk?"

He looked, to Tetra, like a man who would contribute to the delinquency of a minor, but that wasn't necessarily the same thing.

"Perhaps not," she said.

"The original kidnapper is Connell Morgan." The RIC showed no reaction. "I wasn't in on it," Foy hastened to repeat. "I barely know the man. I went to visit him, purely social, and there she was. I mean, I know enough about him to help the police with their inquiries; I can help you put your hands on him right now."

"I am sure you could be very helpful," Tetra said.

"Very helpful. Yes."

"You went to pay a social call and saw the kidnapped woman. And then?"

"Then Morgan called the woman's secretary and told her to clear the Inn. Then they sent me with the message I told you about."

Tetra was up to speed by now. "And you gave it to the Galactic Union agent disguised as a District Criminal Investigator."

"Yes. Then I went back and saw the Stokk. They got in without any noise; somebody must have let them in. I crept up and listened, like I said, and I heard the one introduce himself as Gord Pron, like somebody in there knew him but he was just meeting Morgan for the first time. He said he liked the way somebody — must have been Bel Schuster — had slipped away from the DCI. They talked about how Morgan had messed up a meeting by kidnapping her. He said Freldt Saymak would be a worthy opponent and he was almost sorry she didn't try to work against him with the police. So, naturally, I came looking for the DCI to make a report. I guess he's gone. Lucky for me I found *you* here."

One of Tetra's greatest regrets had always been her physical inability to laugh. It had something to do with the gills, she supposed, but the closest she could ever come was a sort of strangled cough. The series of sounds she made now were so alarming that both Foy and the bartender shouted, "Can you speak? Can you breathe?" She managed to get herself under control.

It's not really funny. Bel's in serious trouble.

Tetra ran through a scenario or two. She could get back aboard the *St. Greg* and tell the Captain all this. The Captain could. . . . The Captain could do nothing. There was still the possibility one of the Grand Council was working with the Stokk against the interests of the Galactic Union and would use this contretemps to make the GU look bad.

But how simple! How obvious! The "Galactic Union agent" disguised as a District Criminal Investigator was, in all likelihood, the *real* District Criminal Investigator; the very Pel Darzin who had arranged to meet Freldt Saymak at the Inn. He had asked about the Stokk. He had known Freldt's name, and he had said he knew where Freldt is. Assuming he didn't really know where Freldt is, he meant he knew the whereabouts of the person he *thought* was Freldt: Bel. And, if he wasn't here anymore, maybe he was where Bel was.

Tetra decided it was high time somebody took hold of this mess and shook it out straight. "Take me to where Bel Schuster is being held," she said. "If you see the agent you spoke to before, point him out."

"Point him out? Don't you know him?"

"Certainly, I know him. I know who the *real* Galactic Union agent is. But you could have spoken to *a false* agent."

Foy shook his head, silenced by this evidence of how far in over his head he had plunged.

Tetra stood and looked down her nose at the bartender. "If Innkeeper Knosh Jok'rel comes looking for me," she said, "please tell him I will return soon. I have to, er, go back to the reservation and milk my elk." To Foy, she said, "Is there a back way out of this place?"

Before the bartender could decide whether she had heard right and the message didn't make sense, or whether the message made sense but she hadn't heard it right, the two left.

~*~

"What do you mean, she said she'd return soon?" Knosh Jok'rel eyed his bartender fishily. "Where did she go?"

"She said she had to go do something."

"Inspect the facilities, maybe? See what we've got available so the shore party doesn't think it has to be stuck in the bar the whole time like it did before?"

"Yes. I guess."

"You guess?"

"That must be what she said. Sure, that's what she said."

"It's a good idea. Let me know when she gets back and I'll tell the Grand Council to call her ship."

"Sure thing."

~*~

Foy led Tetra around and about, ending in an alley.

Tetra felt inordinately pleased with herself. *So far, so good. Now, if I can just manage to get through this without attracting official notice. . . .*

"I beg your pardon," said a uniformed female, stepping into the alley, "but I'm afraid you're both to come with me."

Chapter 23

Gord Pron drew back the bolt. "Let's go, Bookkeeper."

"You fool!" Morgan stepped out of Ligniss' immediate reach. "She's setting us all up! Leaving me here to be savaged, and leading you straight into a trap! I'm not her boyfriend, and she isn't Freldt Saymak, Bookkeeper or otherwise! She's Isobel Enid Schuster of the Galactic Union, probably an agent with the Galactic Planet Rangers!"

"With the what?" Bel liked the sound of it, but enough was enough.

"Don't play the innocent with me, my girl. You said, yourself, you didn't want to get the Space Troopers involved. I admit, you had me fooled. Me!" Morgan laughed a hollow, bitter laugh. "But now I see it. You aren't an 'official' at all. This was all an elaborate plot cooked up between the Rangers and the Llannonninn police. And it almost worked. You almost snared me. But it took the resources of the entire planet and the Galactic Union combined to do it."

Pron said to Bel, "What do you usually do when he gets like this?"

"She isn't Freldt Saymak, I tell you. You were at Jok'rel's. Didn't you see Saymak and the other one go out and come back?"

Pron nodded.

"This is the other one! They switched clothes, you hyperpigmented idiot! I'm not her sweetheart, I abducted her!"

"Yes, but of course—"

"I shudder," said Morgan, doing so, "to think what your love life must be like. The St. Valentine's Day Massacre would hold no irony for you."

"Good one," said Bel.

"I abducted a woman I thought was a Galactic Union official, planning to hold her for ransom. And all the time, she was throwing a net over me."

The Stokk looked as if they thought *someone* ought to throw a net over him.

Bel's mind drifted a bit. *All I wanted was a new outfit and a breath of fresh air. Was that so much to ask?*

Pron's voice was firm but reasonable. "And where is Freldt Saymak, then?"

"Helping the police with their inquiries. This one tricked me into sending a message back to the Galactic Union agent at the Inn: Find Freldt Saymak. And it was you, you fool, who tried to lean on the Bookkeeper, and her working hand-in-glove with the police and the Rangers and probably God." And where was Ernie Foy, come to think of it? Not helping the police, anyone who knew him could be sure.

Pron counted to the base number of his race's mathematical system. Then he spoke, too calmly to be quite sane. "This is true. So many things are clear now. I *have* been a fool." He sneered at Morgan. "But you're a bigger one. Throwing a net over *you*? The Rangers were called in to snare *me*. Me, and the power behind me. Do you think the resources of half the known populated planets would combine to counter the likes of *you*? Only the Stokk are worthy of such an effort! The plan was to lead me to my doom; you only wandered into the path of the blow meant for me."

"Liar! Blackguard!"

"Braggart! Windbag!"

"Boys, boys," said Bel. "Calm down. You're both wrong."

The "boys" turned on her with equally malignant snarls. Utrop Ligniss didn't snarl, though. He just crossed his arms over his chest and smiled. Maybe somebody would have to get smashed, maybe not. Either way, he got paid the same. That was the beauty part of being a strongarm man; you got paid either way.

"I told you," said Morgan, "what would happen to you, if you lied to me."

"No, no," said Bel, spinning another thread, and praying it was strong enough to hold her. "Only if I weren't *valuable* to you, not if I lied. I admit, I did lie, but only to keep down the price of my freedom. You can't blame me, can you?"

Morgan knew his limits. He knew when he'd been blindfolded and twirled until he didn't know a donkey's butt from a doorway to a precipitate flight of stairs, and he knew when it was time to stop being a good sport if he wanted to cop a prize. "Gag her," he said to Ligniss. "Please, before it's too late."

"Shut up," said Pron. "What are you talking about, woman?"

"I am an agent," said Bel, "of the Galactic Union Security Caucus."

"The Security Caucus doesn't have agents," said Morgan.

"I'm a *secret* agent. Naturally, you didn't know they had secret agents, because if everybody knew about us. . . ."

"You wouldn't be secret anymore," said Pron. "Naturally."

"I told you to gag her," said Morgan. "I warned you, but you wouldn't listen; oh, no, you wouldn't listen."

"Someone on the Grand Council suspects a traitor in their midst and appealed to the Caucus for help. They sent me. Before I came here, I knew nothing of any of you gentlemen, nor the powers behind you, nor the horses you rode in on."

"The what?"

"Horses," said Morgan. "They produce what she's shoveling."

"Shut up," said Pron.

"I'll make you a deal," said Bel. "Tell me the name of the traitor, and let me walk, and I'll see to it nobody falls but the Councilor. How does that sound?"

It sounded like another lie to Morgan. He would have said so, but Ligniss had uncrossed his arms and moved within knuckle-dusting distance.

It didn't sound bad to Pron. In fact, only one thing would make it better, and it was the only thing that would make it work.

"Since you've decided to tell me the truth," he said, "I'll tell *you* the truth. I don't know who the Councilor is. But Gunjin Jippir knows. Now, if Gunjin Jippir got deported, I'm in a good position to take over for him. Just until he's allowed to come back, you understand."

"I understand," said Bel, with a heavy wink.

"Ligniss here would be my right hand man, wouldn't you, Ligniss?"

Ligniss shrugged and smiled. Anybody's credits spent the same.

And the delectable Korp Norstu. . . . *There'll be a warm and cozy place in the new organization for her, oh, yes.*

"Say you take out Gunjin Jippir," said Pron, "and get him to take down the Councilor, and say you make the arrangements from here, and you've got a deal."

Bel considered it, but not for long. *Not a good idea.* One wrong word from the other end could lead to very messy complications. Better if she could get the Stokk to take her to the Inn. She might not *be* any safer there, but she would *feel* safer there. If push came to shove, she'd be within the ship's transfer area; Captain Fazzaria could pull her up and leave the villains empty-handed.

"How can I make the arrangements from here? Do you see a phone of any kind?"

"No."

"We'll have to—"

"Squawkbox," said Morgan nastily. "She has a squawkbox on her wrist. She can raise the ship on it."

"Thanks heaps," said Bel.

"My pleasure," said Morgan.

"Raise the ship, then," said Pron. "Tell them my terms."

"Fine," said Bel, hoping everything remained copacetic among the authorities. They had cleared the Inn, so all was well so far. Now, if Captain Fazzaria would just go one step farther and pull Bel out in good enough shape to testify, everyone involved would get a commendation. The capture of the Gunjin guy, apparently some kind of crime kingpin, and the unmasking of a Council collaborator? Yes, commendations would definitely be in order.

"Don't forget *my* terms," said Morgan. "They still stand."

"No, they don't," said Pron. "Just tell them *my* terms. When Gunjin Jippir's been taken, when I hear his voice telling me he's been taken, and what he's going to do to me if he ever gets the chance, then I'll release you." *You hope.*

Bel might have read his mind. *Sure you will.* "They won't go for it. Come with me back to the Inn and offer to finger your boss in return for immunity."

Pron struck the table so hard with the flat of his hand the empty liquor bulbs bounced and rolled. "You dare to dictate terms to me?"

Bel had to smile, for he reminded her strongly of Mother Ignatius Loyola, who had been Dean of St. Bennedetta's when Bel had been a senior. Mother Pugnacious, the kids had called her.

Pron, seeing the smile, straightened and grew quiet.

Bel hoped he had gotten a splinter in his paw, so she could remove it and earn his everlasting gratitude. But he hadn't.

"You're stalling," Pron said. "They know where you are, or they have a good idea where to look. You're trying to keep us occupied—"

Pron came around the table so fast he seemed to have come

through it, and clasped the back of Bel's neck in one hand. The other hand he made into a fist and drew back.

"Call," he said. "You're not much to look at now, but you might improve if I punch your lips off against your teeth."

Morgan, Bel was gratified to hear, objected: "Oh, now, just a minute!"

"Ligniss," said Pron.

Bel heard a scuffle, but she was too busy trying to tame Pron with the power of the human eye to look away.

Ligniss sounded a tiny bit wistful. "Can I crack him this time?"

"Just keep him quiet for now," said Pron. "I'm wondering if he isn't in on the plot, somehow; part of the stall. He may be useful, yet." To Bel, he said, "Call."

Call. Call Tetra again, never mind the fancy work; just give her the facts and the terms. Let the Captain take it from there. Some vacation.

"I'll do it," said Bel, "but you're making a big mistake."

Pron's hand tightened on Bel's neck, then dropped away.

Bel closed her eyes. When she opened them again, Pron was at the door, shooting the bolt.

"You warned me," he said. "Why?"

"I'm a renegade," said Bel, thankful, not for the first time, for her four years as a lecturer (and a listener) at Juliette Women's Correctional Facility, where she had learned lying from the best. "The Caucus sends me in to nail a criminal, right? I nail somebody, and say it's the criminal, right? Somebody backs me up, somebody tones down the operation, I get a big payoff, and everybody's happy, right?"

"Everybody but the somebody who gets nailed," said Pron.

"Life is pain," said Bel. "Now, if I'd made the call you wanted under duress, I'd have given a certain signal, and this place would have been swarming. You wouldn't get anything, I wouldn't get anything."

"The door's bolted now," Pron pointed out. "Give your signal, and you and the stooge over there will be jammer meat before we're taken."

"But you *will* be taken. That's the point you need to consider. But, if you make it worth my while, I'll see you aren't even pulled in for questioning."

Bel had lost track of how many, er, creative realities this one made. Her next confession with Brother Theodore would be a very long one. Maybe she could talk him into just baptizing her again and starting fresh next week.

"Make it worth your while. . . . Yes, I see a way. Look, the whole plan here is for the Bookkeeper to get Jok'rel to turn over the Inn to Gunjin Jippir, right?"

"Right."

"But Gunjin Jippir won't be around to have anything turned over to him, will he?"

"I'm afraid not," said Bel. "Too bad."

"Send Jok'rel over, too, and see to it the franchise comes to me. And to you as my silent partner. You, see?"

"Silent partner," said Morgan. "Ouch!"

"Easy, Ligniss," said Pron. "Put him down, and give your arms a rest."

"My arms aren't tired," said Ligniss, but he did as he was told.

Bel kept her eyes on Pron. "What's my cut?"

"Ten percent."

"I'm awfully sorry, but I'm a trifle deaf in one ear. How much did you say?"

"Twenty. With a Galactic Union contract, and increased business from improved relations, twenty percent won't be too shabby."

"Not even after you skim off the cream?"

Pron laughed. "Let's say thirty, then."

"Let's say fifty, and if I see thirty, I won't kick."

"How do I know I can trust you?"

"Because there's something in it for me," Bel explained. "How do I know I can trust *you*?"

"Same reason."

"That'll have to do, I guess. Well, let's go."

Pron shook his head. "From here. And watch those signals. Anybody swarms us, they'll need electron microscopes to pick up all your pieces."

Bel raised her arm, her courage, and her eyes unto the Lord. She activated the squawkbox.

Chapter 24

After Tetra, dressed in her black-and-silver power suit, left locus B15 on her peacekeeping assignment, the Crisis Team returned to their discussion.

"The Stokk will be calling with his ransom demands," said Captain Fazzaria; for, it will be remembered, it was Gord Pron whom Freldt Saymak supposed had Bel in the first place.

Quatro, who prided himself on his lack of curiosity, was nevertheless the one who asked first. "Will you comply?"

"It depends on what they are," said Jinx. "On the whole, I doubt it."

"Then," said Dr. Frazni, "you plan to abandon Ven Schuster to her fate?"

"You can't say she didn't ask for it," said Hessaphess. "If I told her once, I told her half-a-dozen times: Don't leave the Inn. Don't leave the Inn."

"That will do, Ven Hessaphess," said Jinx. "Dr. Frazni, I dislike the idea of deserting a crewmember, perhaps more than you do." *After all, I'm the one who'll have to explain it to Sector Command, not to mention the Jesuits.* "I hope it won't be necessary, but you must see the impossibility of bowing to criminal threats. The Galactic Union cannot—"

"Captain," said First Mate Harry Chestney, "request permission to—"

"Request denied."

"There's one thing we haven't yet considered, Captain," said Quatro.

"Enlighten me."

"Why did the Stokk call us with a ransom demand?"

"Because they have. . . . Because they think they have. . . . Good question."

"What's good about it?" Hessaphess wasn't forgetting who had started this mess. "Who would they *expect* to pay ransom for Schuster? Holy Mother Church? Although they might come closer to getting something for her there."

"Flippancy is a counter-productive way of dealing with emotions too painful to confront," said Dr. Frazni, patting Hessaphess's large red hand with his own slender silvered one. "It also wastes time."

"What I meant," said Quatro, "is this: If the Stokk think they've captured Freldt Saymak, the Bookkeeper, we wouldn't figure in their thinking at all. If they know they have one of our Professors. . . ."

Hessaphess completed the question. ". . .what would give them the idea she's worth ransoming? I see what you mean. Well, it's obvious, isn't it? She's been at it. They got hold of her, and she cooked up some tale and puffed up her own importance, and you see where it's led."

"It would be inconsistent with Ven Schuster's personnel record and scan patterns," said Dr. Frazni, "for her to 'cook up a tale' which would increase her danger. Her actual value to these people is nil; her past record suggests she would, in this case, tell the literal truth. If she hasn't, it must be because the literal truth is more dangerous than any lie she might have told, or seemed to be at the time she told it."

"In other words," said Jinx, "there's more to this than we realize." *Comforting thought.*

An uneasy silence ensued, during which Fazzaria, Hessaphess, and Frazni affected to be catching up on discwork, Quatro Petrie graded a quantity of tests, and Chestney improved on his best score in a series of Deathpawn chess combat games.

The Crisis Team jumped in unison as the intercom sounded.

"Fazzaria here," said Jinx.

"Captain," said Donna Meichi, "I have another unauthorized transmission from Council City on Llannonn. This one's from Bel Schuster, too. She wants to talk to Tetra Petrie again. It's coming from within the parameters you gave me; the computer's locking onto it now."

"Did you tell her Ven Petrie had transferred to Jok'rel's?"

"No, Captain. Did you want me to?"

"No, thank you. Just put her through to me here."

"Yes, Captain."

Jinx, bearing Dr. Frazni's analysis in mind, determined to give Bel some room to maneuver and see what she made of it. It was an eerie reversal of the natural order. Jinx didn't like it.

~*~

"Tetra?"

"We've been waiting to hear from you," said Jinx. "What's taken you so long?"

Bel would have known Jinx's voice from Tetra's, even without the contractions. Was Tetra helping to clear Jok'rel's, where Foy had delivered the message to "Find Freldt Saymak?" *Had* they found Freldt Saymak?

Bel darted a look at Morgan, afraid he might notice the substitution, but he was too far away from the squawkbox to hear anything but noise.

Pron was close, though, close enough to do serious damage before a word misspoken could be covered or retrieved.

Bel chose her words with care. "Is Freldt Saymak all right?"

"Freldt Saymak?" So the Stokk knew they'd missed their intended victim. "Yes," Jinx said. Then, tentatively, she said, "Do they know who you are?"

"Yes," Bel said quickly. "I had to tell them. I've been threatened with everything from enslavement to an outpatient lipectomy. I had to tell them I'm an agent of the Galactic Union Security Caucus, and that I came to Llannonn because somebody on the Grand Council suspects one of the Councilors of working with the Stokk."

"You did?"

"Yeah. They're willing to trade. They'll release me unharmed and testify against their boss, who can name the Grand Councilor he's working with. In return, they want Jok'rel's Traveler's Rest Inn franchise and immunity. Sound fair?"

"It doesn't matter what it sounds like to me," said the Captain. Maybe she could draw out the contact long enough for Donna Meichi to locate the source. What good it would do, she didn't know. "I can't make such a decision. I'll have to clear it. That'll take time."

Pron leaned over Bel's shoulder. "She doesn't have time," he said. "I want your answer now."

"I can give you an answer," said Jinx, "but it won't stick. I have to clear it, I tell you."

"Tracing the call," said Morgan. "They're tracing the call. We're going to get swarmed, and you're going to dice us. Break it off!"

"Clear it," said Pron. "You have one standard hour."

Bel broke contact. *Could be worse. The Captain played up like a good'un.* It would have been easy to trace the call, given the limits Bel had passed in her previous message. Captain Fazzaria would clear Pron's demands with the Grand Council, even the traitor would pretend to be outraged and would vote to accept the terms in order to cover *being* the traitor, and a squad of police would surround Morgan's to assure her safe release.

Help was on the way.

~*~

"Do you think that's true?" Harry glanced around the table, looking for opinions. "Do you think she's really sold them about being an agent? Are they really willing to help us get this Councilor?"

The Captain answered. "What does it matter? There's nothing we can do about it."

"We can tell the Grand Council."

"And the Councilor the Stokk are offering to help expose can turn the whole thing against us and claim this whole episode is a plot between the Stokk and the Galactic Union to disrupt the Llannonninn government. It isn't as if we have a close working relationship with the Llannonninn authorities. And, if we go to them with this, we'll have an awful lot that'll weigh against us."

"Nothing so bad, surely," said Chestney.

Jinx ticked off the points on her fingers. "We have a staff member off-limits. We have a Llannonninn native aboard, against her will. We have a major movement, with at least one Grand Councilor in the membership, strongly against off-worlder involvement in Llannonninn affairs. And we very nearly created an inter-galactic incident within three hours of setting foot on the planet."

Hessaphess shifted uneasily.

"But," said Chestney, "the Stokk and the Galactic Union? We're enemies."

"Nobody has enemies anymore," said Hessaphess. "Get with the times, Chestney."

"Adversaries," Chestney corrected himself. "Traditionally and by nature."

"But the Stokk are off-worlders, and so are we," said Jinx. "The Llannonn for the Llannonninn party would enter us all in the same database."

"Then what did you mean, when you said you'd clear it?"

"Sector Command," said Quatro. "I hadn't thought of Sector Command. We, on the faculty, tend to forget that you, in the military portion of the staff, have resources beyond those available aboard ship. Naturally, you'll contact them for instructions."

Jinx had been hoping no one had thought of Sector Command. She bent to inspect the jagged remnants of her nails in order to hide the look of loathing she would otherwise have cast at the professor.

Hessaphess expressed her concern for her. "Contact SecCom? Let them know what kind of debacle Schuster's made of a simple shore leave, and get all our cans transferred to point duty in the Stokk/Union DMZ? No, thank you."

"Well put, Ven Hessaphess," said the Captain. "Precisely. And," she continued, as Quatro and Frazni opened their mouths to protest, their cans not being available to Sector Command for point duty, "the Troopers wouldn't appreciate being told, either, not unless absolutely necessary. What they don't know, they don't have to acknowledge. If we can deal with this ourselves, fine. If we can't, their next expectation would be for us to find a rug to sweep it under and make with the broom."

Hessaphess and Chestney nodded in unison, like an unmatched pair of hover-car ornaments with springs in their necks.

"Then, as I asked before," said the Empathetic Diagnostician, "you plan to abandon Professor Schuster?"

Jinx took a deep breath and faced the fact. "If I must," she said. "And, if I must, I'll require you to wipe all memory of this incident from the mind of our Llannonninn guest, as I believe Professor Petrie has already suggested. I see you find the prospect distasteful, but the only alternative is for us to take her with us when we go and lose her somewhere on the way."

"You wouldn't, Captain," said Frazni, unimpressed with the threat. "Remember, I've studied *your* personnel record and scan patterns, as well."

"But you do understand—"

Frazni nodded, and waved a long slim hand. "I do," he said. "Although, as you say, I find the prospect distasteful."

"I've been thinking, Captain," said Quatro, as if this meant they could all relax now. "Our period of grace is very nearly up. The Stokk will be calling again, to see if you're willing to accede to his demands."

"Yes," said Jinx, feeling her nickname never more appropriate.

"Suppose we do?"

The Captain stared blankly at the professor, wondering which one of them had skipped a groove this time.

"Suppose we do what?"

"Suppose we tell him we agree. Tell him we've cleared it, and we're willing to give him anything he wants. Tell him to bring Ven Schuster to Jok'rel's, along with whatever story he plans to tell against his employer and the Llannonninn Innkeeper. Tell him we'll call in the police to take his statement when he's certain we're acting in good faith."

"But," said Jinx. "We can't."

"Naturally," said Quatro, "we *won't* be acting in good faith. By the time he calls again, to tell us he's in place, Tetra will have returned with the lifting of our interdiction from communications and transference between the ship and the Inn. We can pull Ven Schuster up, send Freldt Saymak down, break orbit, and let them all sort it out between themselves."

"Lie." Jinx wondered why she hadn't thought of it herself.

"If you have some irrational scruples against it," said Quatro, "let Hessaphess do it. He won't mind."

"Here, now," said Hessaphess.

"Nor would I," said Quatro, making it clear he had meant the charge as a compliment.

Chestney nodded. "What've we got to lose?"

That, Jinx feared, was something they had yet to learn.

Chapter 25

Tetra and Foy gazed upon Ruah Maeek with eyes so wide and innocent, the officer had to fight the illusion she saw them painted on black velvet.

Foy blinked guilelessly. "Come with you? I don't understand."

Tetra remained still and silent, perhaps hoping to be overlooked.

"Accompany me from this spot to another," said Officer Maeek. "Both of you. In custody. Mine. Now do you understand?"

Foy laughed. "You're collaring *her*?" He shoved a finger toward Tetra.

"In addition to you," said the officer.

"Don't you know who she is?"

"This is one of the things we plan to ask her, I expect."

"Tell her," Foy said to the language professor. "Tell her who she's trying to take."

"I do not think 'trying' is the applicable word," said Tetra. "Officer, what laws have we broken?" It was too much to hope that the answer would be "none."

"None," said Officer Maeek. "None we know of. District Criminal Investigator Pel Darzin has some questions for you."

"Just the man we want to see!" Foy had never thought to hear himself say any such thing. "Lead us to him."

Tetra went in some trepidation. Taking hold of this mess and shaking it out straight didn't seem quite so manifest a destiny as it had in the security of the Inn.

As Officer Maeek escorted her charges out of the alley, Foy and Darzin pointed at one another and said, "You!"

"So!" Foy shook with rage. "I knew it! It's a plot!" He clutched at Officer Maeek's tunic.

"That'll be enough of that," she said sternly.

Foy transferred his grip to his own lapels, and said, "It's a plot, I tell you! They're all in it, and they're trying to pin it on me! All I did was deliver the message!"

He turned to Tetra, wringing his hands so vigorously some of the ick flaked off of them. "As soon as I heard about the plot, I came to you, didn't I? Tell them I did."

"He did," said Tetra.

"And who are you?" Darzin wondered, *Could it be?* "And who is this man, really? And what is he talking about?"

"Let me ask you first," said Tetra. "Are you District Criminal Investigator Pel Darzin?"

"I am. And this is Communications Commission Official Darlla Bute. Officer Ruah Maeek, you've met. Officer Ander Patth."

Darlla Bute introduced her BLITS team, the driver and the man on the monitors waving from inside the van.

"And you?" Darzin asked again.

"But," said Foy, "if you're District Criminal Investigator Pel Darzin, you must know who she is." A terrible suspicion hit again. "You aren't a Regional Investigative Coordinator," he accused Tetra.

"A what?"

"You told me you're a Regional Investigative Coordinator."

"I told you no such thing."

"You let me think—"

"I did not know what you thought. I am not psychic."

"You're in on it! I should have known!" He shook his fists and sank into morose contemplation.

"I think I do know who she is," said Darzin. He held out his thumb. "'Bel,'" he said. "I have so much to ask you."

"So do we all," said Tetra. "But I am not Bel, either."

"Then. . . . Where is she? And who are you? And. . . ."

Tetra found herself faced with a situation she hadn't been in since her forbidden pet barracuda had torn up the neighbors' coral beds: How much, if any, of the truth to tell. She decided now, as she had then, that some was necessary, but least was best.

"Bel Schuster is in there, held captive by Stokk criminals."

"As I told you," Darzin said to Bute.

"You said it was Bookkeeper Freldt Saymak," she said.

"It's both of them," said Foy. "And they aren't being held captive, they're conspiring."

Tetra had an uneasy moment, wondering if this could, in any degree, be true. She decided, even so, it was impractical at this point to admit the possibility.

"You *would* say that," she said.

Darzin gave Foy a just-as-I-suspected look and said, "Turncoat! She gives you the opportunity to help your planet and you have no more faith in her than this."

"Shame!" Officers Patth and Maeek shook their index fingers at Foy.

"Help my planet?"

"He does not know any better," said Tetra.

"Oh, I understand," said Darzin. "She didn't tell him everything, eh?"

"I rather doubt it," said Tetra. "How much did she tell *you*, District Criminal Investigator Pel Darzin?"

"She sent me a warning, by him, and a message."

"'Find Freldt Saymak,'" said Foy, bitterly. "Fool that I am. And all of you knowing very well she had rendezvoused here with the rest of the gang. Serves me right for doing something honest. I'll know better in the future."

Darzin shushed him. "Will you be quiet? But how did it happen? How did Bel get in there?"

"She—" Foy began, but Tetra unfortunately trod upon his toe and spoke before he could complicate things further.

"She changed places with the Bookkeeper in the Inn," said Tetra. "And led the Stokk away from her."

Darzin was speechless. *The courage! The nobility!* "Then where is Freldt Saymak?"

"She's in there, I tell you," said Foy. "I heard them call her by name!"

"Mistaken identity," said Tetra. "It happens all the time. As for where Freldt Saymak is now, I could not say."

"In hiding," Darzin suggested, "until it's safe for her to appear."

"Exactly," said Tetra.

"And the illegal transmission," said Darlla Bute, who had been waiting for an opening with the patience of a you-know-what. "Made from that house. Made by whom?"

"I could not say," said Tetra.

"Apparently," said Darlla Bute, "you also cannot say your name. For the last time, who are you? What are you doing here? Who is this man? What is he doing here? —You perceive the general drift of my questioning."

"Yes. Well." There was nothing for it. A bit more of the feline would have to protrude from the encasing material. "I am from the Galactic Union ship now in orbit. The *St. Gregory the Wonderworker*. Eleven of us transferred to Jok'rel's for a shore leave. While there, Bel Schuster and Freldt Saymak made the change I mentioned earlier. We were recalled and, in leaving, our Duty Officer inadvertently insulted the Innkeeper. The Captain sent me to make our apologies."

Darzin nodded. *Nice cover.*

Darlla Bute regarded him with admiration. "This makes sense to you?"

"After I had done so," Tetra continued, "this man," she waved a hand at Foy, who bared his teeth at her, "came in and told me Bel Schuster had been kidnapped, and is now in the power of the criminal Stokk I also mentioned earlier."

"Couldn't be clearer," said Darzin.

Bute was not to be sidetracked. "Who made the call?"

Foy would have foamed at the mouth if his caps hadn't gotten in the way. "Bel! I saw her do it! She called her secretary, Tetra, and told her she'd been taken. Told her to clear the Inn—" He goggled. "You're Tetra! You're the Galactic Union agent!"

All eyes fastened upon the Gilhoolie woman.

Darzin's twinkled. He hadn't had to be told the whoabouts of the woman in black. Not *the* Galactic Union agent, but *a* Galactic Union agent, and not the chief one, either. The hand of a genius showed in this, and he knew whose: Code name, "Bel."

Darla Bute addressed Tetra sternly. "Is this true? —And if you tell us one more time you could not say, I'll run you in so fast your shadow won't know where you went."

"Colorful," said Tetra.

"ComCom Official Darlla Bute!" The man monitoring the van's equipment called to her. "We're picking up another illegal transmission."

"From here?"

"Yes."

"Probably the call I said I'm expecting," said Darzin. "From the Stokk. If it is, the station house will patch it through to me here."

This is where the plan would begin to unfold. The Stokk would call with the deal. Darzin would promise silence in return for "Freldt's" safety. The Stokk would release their captive; she would bring them up on charges, not with the corrupted Grand Council, but with the Galactic Union Security Caucus. Under the harsh light of disinterested inquiry, the Stokk and their pet Councilor would have no place to hide.

The DCI rested a finger on the "receive" key and held his breath.

In a moment, the man in the van called, "Transmission over."

Darzin looked at his mobile unit as if it had struck him from behind.

"That's it, then," said Bute. "We're going in."

Darzin held out a hand. "No, please! If you storm the place, who knows what the Stokk might do to Bel?"

"Who is this Bel?"

Darzin looked at Tetra, who flicked her eyes to Bute and back, winked, and shook her head. If the DCI didn't pick up the signal, she could always claim a nervous tick. She felt herself on the verge of developing one, anyway.

"Bel is your perpetrator," said Darzin, "and she's my witness. We need her intact."

"This is true," said Bute. "What do you suggest?"

"Arrest everybody!" Foy straightened his hat and said, "Everybody but me, I mean. I heard what I heard."

"We seem to have some confusion," said Darzin, "as to exactly who is up there and exactly what they're doing." He turned to Foy. "What's the layout inside?"

"A stairway just inside the door. It leads up to a landing. The upstairs door was closed when I heard what I heard. It's usually kept locked."

"You have a key?"

"No."

"A password?"

"A knock. One long, two short, four long."

"Good." He spoke to Bute. "We'll send her up—"

"Him, you mean," Bute said, indicating Foy.

"I mean her," Darzin said, indicating Tetra. "The Galactic Union . . . er . . . Emissary."

Send me up. They'll send me up for life, before this is over. This was not one of my better ideas. It occurred to Tetra she might have been spending too much time with the irrepressible

Tsung Li, after all.

"She can represent herself as . . . as. . . ."

"I will think of something," said Tetra.

"How do we know we can trust her?"

Darzin felt nothing but contempt for Bute's narrow attitude. *Probably a Llannonn for the Llannonninnite.* Well, if she couldn't see what he could see, he wasn't going to waste time drawing her a graphic.

"We can send one of my officers with her," he said, veiling the look of withering scorn he so longed to flash. "She can go in and speak loudly, and the officer can stand outside the door and listen. When it's clear who and what we have to deal with, we can decide how to handle it."

"Let's decide one thing right now," said Darlla Bute. "I *am* going to make an arrest. Somebody's been making illegal transmissions and, whether it's this Bel person or your mother's prize pratty, I'll take *somebody* to court."

"Understood," said Darzin. He smiled as he visualized the look on ComCom Official Darlla Bute's face when the whole, true story came out.

"I'm glad you're amused," Bute went on. "I'll also take *you* to court, District Criminal Investigator Pel Darzin, for your infraction of departmental procedures."

"That's only right," Darzin admitted. "But I think even you will have to agree I was justified."

"Could we talk about this later?" Tetra was as antsy as Quatro, the time a student had put itching powder inside the professor's wig. If the illegal call hadn't been the Stokk offering to let somebody go, it had certainly been *something*. While she wished the next sound she heard would be somebody's voice saying, "And then she woke up," she knew it would not be. The only way to get out of this one was to go the rest of the way through it.

"Yes, of course," said Darzin. "I need an officer. . . ."

"I volunteer!" Officer Ander Patth stood sharply to attention. If Darzin went to court for having a mobile unit without permission, the man who requisitioned the unit would go, too. Just as well to take a citation for heroism in with him.

"Good man," said Darzin. "Quietly, now."

Tetra led the way with catlike tread.

Chapter Five, thought Officer Ander Patth, *Stairway to Danger.*

Chapter 26

The door handle turned and the door pressed in upon its bolt. Gord Pron flattened himself against the wall near the hinges and said to Bel, "Get close and say something."

Bel had watched enough cop shows and gangster movies to get the idea, and the look she cast the extortionist as she approached the door was one of deep reproach.

"Who is it?" She hoped the portal didn't burst asunder, and herself with it.

There was an extended pause, while Tetra, outside, made the lowering discovery she wasn't creative under pressure. Then a muffled voice said, "Candygram."

"What?"

"Delivery for occupant."

"Tell 'em to leave it," Pron whispered.

"Leave it," said Bel.

"I cannot. Somebody will have to sign for it."

"Tetra?"

"Bel?"

"You know this person?" Pron edged up to the peephole and looked out. "There's no one there."

"That's Tetra."

Pron shoved Bel away from the door and eased back the bolt. He pulled the door open, snagged the startled Gilhoolie, and dragged her into the room. He slammed and bolted the door behind her.

"Tetra! Am I ever glad to see you!"

"With what justification?"

"The Captain sent you, didn't she? With some kind of guarantee from the Grand Council to accept the Stokk's terms for my release?"

"The Captain sent me," Tetra agreed.

"They didn't dally," said Pron. "Bel must be one of the Security Caucus' top agents."

"Uh," said Tetra.

There's something wrong about Tetra. Something's missing. Bel closed her eyes, visualizing how Tetra should look, and opened them again. *Of course!* She wasn't wearing a ribbon.

"What happened to the old woman?"

"She simply decided it would be best for me to come."

"Not the Captain, the old—"

"Tetra! I remember that name," said Morgan. "She's your secretary! Then it's true!"

"Why, Connell," said Bel, in order to cover Tetra's confusion, "did you think I would lie, with my life on the line? Perhaps you don't realize what dangerous, murderous people these Stokk are, but I do. Tetra does, too, don't you, Tetra?"

"I do now," said Tetra, weakly. Then, rather louder, she said, "You mean these two Stokk here? This yellow one and this pink one? They are threatening your life, Bel Schuster? And the life of this man with very large feet? As there is no one else in the room, I can only assume this is what you mean."

Pron made a stab at recovering control of the conversation. "Where's the package?"

"Package?" Tetra looked around, but saw no package.

"The package. For occupant. I take it you referred to the guarantees Bel mentioned."

"Do you?" Tetra stalled, unwilling to throw any bull until she knew where she was stepping.

"Just a set of passwords," said Bel. "To let her know I'm all right. Having a package to sign for is code meaning the deal hasn't been cleared yet, but they're working on it."

"Yes, of course," said Pron. "I knew that."

"How are the negotiations going?" Bel was almost afraid to ask.

"I know nothing about it," said Tetra. "I was in the Inn when a greasy-looking man came in—"

"Foy," said Bel. "With my message. I understand. Say no more about it."

Pron laughed. "Much good it did you," he said. "I was too clever for you, wasn't I?"

"You were too something for me, that's for sure." Bel didn't know Tetra well, but she'd seen enough unprepared students in her time to recognize somebody who hadn't a clue. She could tell, from the look Tetra gave her now, the Gilhoolie knew one when she saw one, too.

Something had to be done. She and Tetra couldn't stand here warning one another off subjects for long without somebody tumbling to it. She had to think of some other way, some code, for them to communicate at least a few indispensable snatches of information.

"This had better not be a trick," said Pron. "Remember what I said would happen to you, if we got swarmed."

"What would happen?" Tetra had to ask.

Pron smiled at Ligniss. Ligniss smiled at Tetra and pantomimed breaking something in two and tossing the pieces in different directions.

"No one will come bursting in here," Tetra projected. "Do not worry you will be forced to do something violent."

"All right, all right," said Gord Pron. "You don't have to shout."

"That is what you think," Tetra muttered.

Bel thought again of what she knew of Tetra. Professor of Linguistics. . . . Reader of Catholic instructional materials.

"Speaking of negotiations," Bel said to Tetra, "am I right in assuming the vallums have aurises?"

"The vallums have aurises?"

"You know, like *Domini Patri* has?"

"*Domini Patri*. . . ." Tetra got it. Latin. The vallums. . . . The walls have ears. "Yes. Sort of like Miles."

Sort of like Miles. Soldier. Sort of like soldier. . . . Police. The police are listening.

"Looks like a Mexican standoff for now," she said.

"Well," said Pron, "whoever this guy Mexican is, he'd better not stand off too long; your time is running out."

"We are on the clock?"

Pron's hard black eyes narrowed. "You should know."

"Them and their top-hush," said Bel. "How are we supposed to function when they do this to us? How do they know what we'll need to know in the field? I mean, really!"

Tetra had a burst of inspiration. "Remember Esdraelon?"

That one took Bel back so far so fast she nearly blacked out from the trip. *Father Michael's fifth grade Bible History class.* Father Michael was a war buff, and his class had consisted entirely of the strategies and tactics of Old Testament battles, many of which had taken place on the plain of Esdraelon.

"Are Esdraelon's experiences applicable here?"

"I am afraid so," said Tetra.

Bel wasn't madly keen about the idea of tangling with the Stokk, not to mention not knowing which side of the fence Morgan would come down on.

Maybe she could influence his trajectory.

"I just want there to be no mistake about Connell," she said. "He's been so brave and strong through all of this; I don't know what I would have done without him."

"I have? You don't?"

"I knew he was part of it," said Pron.

"Connell stopped him when he threatened to hit me," said Bel. "I won't forget it. When we're safely out of this, I promise you, I won't forget it."

Connell twirled the ends of his mustache, a golden glint in his sapphire eyes.

So much for Morgan. The next step was to take the edge off the Stokk. After all, she and Tetra didn't need to pop anybody's wadding; they only needed to unbolt the door.

"Anyone for a drink while we're waiting? Tetra, how about a Judith Thirteen-Two?"

Judith. . . . One of the books of their Bible. Fortunately, Tetra had read their Bible, and had, as usual, retained most of what she had read. Judith 13:2: *"Judith was left alone in the tent with Holofernes, who lay prostrate on his bed, for he was sodden with wine."* "I am with you," she said aloud.

"Not a bad idea," said Pron. "But none of that liquor stuff for me."

"Me either," said Ligniss. "Got any *hedellma*?"

"I have milk," said Morgan. "Practically the same thing." Into the ensuing silence, he said, "I have it on my cereal, okay?"

"I'll be Mother," said Bel, putting the used liquor bulbs in the sink and assembling ingredients on the drainboard. "Now, sometimes milk is hard for non-Earthlings to digest, so we dilute it with water. Russian water," she added, with a meaningful look at Tetra.

Russian for water. Vada? — Vodka. "I will have a Shirley Temple," she said.

"Same for me," said Bel. "How about you, Connell?"

"Anything," he said. "Excuse me a moment, won't you?"

"Everybody stays in here," said Pron.

"I have to . . . you know." Connell edged toward the door to the inside room. "The facilities."

"You can wait," said Pron, taking his liquor bulb. "Come and drink your Shirley Temple like a man."

"I propose a toast," said Bel. "To success!"

"To success!"

Everyone drank.

"By Krig," said Pron, "this milk-and-water isn't bad, is it, Ligniss?"

"Pretty tasty," the strongarm man agreed.

"Another toast," said Tetra. "To diplomacy."

"Here's to it!" Pron laughed.

"Wait a minute," said Bel. She busied herself at the sink and brought a brimming bowl to the table. "Help yourselves, boys," she said. "A little Mother Russia never hurt anybody."

The Stokk sucked their bulbs dry and stuck the nozzles into the bowl for refills.

"This is very refreshing," said Pron. "How's the time?"

Morgan raised his bulb. "To Stokk!"

"To Stokk!"

Ligniss began to sniffle.

Gord Pron giggled. "He'll be singing *Hit Me Again, Mother,* in a minute," he said.

"'S a byootiful song," said Ligniss, pushing up the sleeves of his gray samtal. "You wanna make something of it?"

Bel was charmed. With any luck, Ligniss would knock the socks off his buddy and sit down to try to harmonize with himself. She began to inch around the table.

Unfortunately, Pron was one of those revolting people whose brains drift in and out of focus when under the influence and, also unfortunately, his brain chose this moment to focus, lock, and zoom.

"Ligniss!" He made a lucky grab for Bel's left arm and gripped it with both hands. "Catch the other one! They're trying to get away!"

Like automatons worked by one master control, Bel and Tetra aimed their liquor bulbs at their captors' eyes and squeezed.

Pron released his hold and Ligniss missed his.

Bel reached the door first, unbolted it and threw it open.

"Help! Police! *Agggk!*"

The "*agggk*" came when Pron gripped her collar and jerked her backwards.

She picked up the no-longer-brimming bowl from the table, sloshed its contents toward Ligniss' face, and broke the bowl over Pron's head.

He let her go again, and folded like a tent.

Force of Habit

Tetra moved fast, but Ligniss had her outmatched in stride. He caught her before she reached the door. Shaking Mother Russia from his dark blue locks, he reeled her in.

It was not for nothing, though, that Tetra had practiced Daoist shadow-boxing for five years. She aimed a kick at Ligniss' knee. She would have hit it, too, if he hadn't lowered his body, preparatory to crushing her against his rocky chest.

Bel and Tetra stared at one another over the fallen forms of their attackers, listening to the sweet sound of flat feet on the stairs.

In the back room, a door slammed.

"I guess he could not wait," said Tetra.

Bel knew him better. "There must be another way out! Maybe we can get back to the Inn and call the ship. They can't arrest us if they can't find us."

"I am right behind you," said Professor Petrie.

The bathroom and closet doors hung open. Bel lunged at the closed door, praying Morgan hadn't stopped to lock it from outside.

He hadn't. She and Tetra half-tumbled down a rickety staircase that made the one at the front of the house look like the approach to the throne.

Bel spotted Morgan half-way up the block, strolling; trying to look nonchalant.

On the theory that any path Morgan took voluntarily was likely to be a path away from prosecution, the women followed.

~*~

Officer Ander Patth was reporting Tetra's listing of the people in the room above when the sound of breaking crockery and falling bodies interrupted him.

"Do you mind if we go in now?" Darlla Bute asked the question of Darzin, with unbecoming sarcasm.

The officers and the BLITS team pounded up the stairs.

~*~

179

On the next street over, a man and two women sauntered off, unchallenged.

So did Foy.

Chapter 27

Connell Morgan prided himself on knowing when the getting was good. When Pron and Ligniss began tussling with the Galactic Union agents, he knew the getting was as good as it would ever be. He eased out of the kitchen. When he heard Bel call for the cops, he scooted across the empty inner room.

He nearly dropped the keys in his hurry, but he had the door unlocked and behind him within seconds. Normally, he would have relocked the door, to slow down possible pursuit. Between the Stokk and the Force, though, it seemed unlikely there would be anyone left to pursue him.

Once on the street, Morgan dropped into an easy walk and stuck his hands in his pockets. He whistled a merry air, and smiled and nodded to all he passed.

He wasn't as unconcerned as he affected to be. In fact, he was downright shaken. Stokk. Dishonest Grand Councilors. Galactic Union secret agents. These dangerous elements had played no part in the simple, harmless Forcible Detention for the Purpose of Extorting Monies he had had in mind.

As for his victim, well, she hadn't really been a victim, had she? Pretending to be what she wasn't; taking advantage of people's trust; tricking them into doing things against their own best interests— Honest people didn't do such things. *Morgan* did such things; his victims were supposed to stand still and be fleeced.

And what a shocking liar the woman had been! And how sweet she had looked, with that blue bow in her hair.

Morgan thought of her in the grip of Gord Pron. *Better her than me.*

Now what to do? Even if no one survived the melee back there long enough for the police to take a statement, Ernie Foy could put the finger on his former partner. Be glad to, to atone for his own part in the proceedings. *The Galactic Union's after me, too. Probably the entire Stokk colony on Llannonn, as well.*

Maybe he could sneak out of the city. Once on the back roads, he could hitch rides to another District, steal some ID papers and some money, and buy passage somewhere on a tramp starship.

At the end of the block Morgan glanced over his shoulder. Bel and Tetra kept pace with him, without even a bruise or tattered garment to show what they'd been up to.

He walked faster but, if ever a man's back spoke of horror coupled indivisibly with despair, Morgan's back so spoke.

Although he couldn't hear them, Bel and Tetra, in unison, said to each other:

Like one that on a lonesome road
Doth walk in fear and dread,
And having once turned round, walks on,
And turns no more his head;
Because he knows a frightful fiend
Doth close behind him tread.

Then Tetra said, "Coleridge," and Bel said, "Burma Shave."

Tetra was right.

Morgan saw someone he knew; one of his former customers. He greeted the man with a great deal more enthusiasm than the man returned.

The professors took the opportunity to catch up.

Morgan turned to them with the look of one who's had enough. "What? What do you want from me?"

"What's the matter with you?" Morgan's former customer came to the women's defense. "They aren't doing anything."

"They're after me, I tell you." To Bel, he said, "Let me go. You said yourself, I saved you from getting your face smashed." To Tetra, he said, "And what have I ever done to you?"

"Never mind me," said Tetra. "I am just with her."

"All I want now is directions to Jok'rel's," said Bel.

"Oh, yes, very likely," said Morgan. "Then it'll be an All Points Bulletin for yours truly."

If she ever got back to Jok'rel's, the last thing Bel intended to do was notify the police. "I hardly think so," she said. "But what's the difference, anyway? You're wanted *now*, aren't you? What's another complaint going to matter to you?"

"As if you didn't intend to see me prosecuted to the fullest extent of the law. As if I had any hope of acquittal, with your testimony against me."

"Well, run along, then," said Bel. "I'll ask this gentleman for directions. You make a getaway while I'm otherwise occupied. You're very good at getaways."

Morgan ran a sweaty hand through his salt-and-pepper curls. "You'd like me to run, wouldn't you?" He darted furtive glances all around, and lowered his voice to a whisper. "You think I don't realize you have people waiting to pick up the tail when you drop off? How big a fool do you take me for?"

"I have yet to get your measure," said Bel.

"Is he in trouble?" Morgan's former customer sounded not at all surprised.

"A bit," said Bel. "Kidnapping, extortion, grievous bodily harm—"

"I never did!"

Bel parted her hair and showed Tetra and the gentleman the lump still on her head from her collision with the alley wall.

"You poor little thing," said the gentleman.

"Poor little thing," said Morgan. "Cold-blooded, stone-hearted, double-dealing little lump of poison. Reminds me of What's-her-name — Medea."

Morgan's former customer drew himself up with dignity. "May I remind you," he said, "that you are speaking of the woman I love?"

Too late, Morgan remembered in what capacity he had served the offended gentleman, and why the Grecian sorceress had sprung so readily to mind: He had sold the gentleman the matched-set names "Medea and Jason Argonaut" for himself and his bride-to-be.

"I beg your pardon," he said. "I do beg your pardon."

But the damage was done. The man looked at Morgan, then deliberately turned his face away. And he meant it to sting.

Morgan felt all security, all help, all hope whirling away like calendar pages in a "time passes" film montage.

He held his wrists out toward Bel. "All right," he said. "I give up. You've got me."

"But I don't want you," said Bel. "Go away and let this man tell us how to get to Jok'rel's. Go on, now. Shoo!"

"No!" Morgan wrung his hands. "You can't do this to me, not after all we've been through together today! You can't just walk off, and leave me to the mercies of whoever the Caucus sends to bring me in. Can't we go somewhere and talk about it, at least?"

"How about Jok'rel's?"

The former customer curled his upper lip. "The place for this one," he said, "is the Bird on a Barseat."

"Is it close?"

"Down two blocks, turn left, the middle of the block."

"Let's go," said Bel.

"Time," Tetra commented.

"Directions," Bel replied in an undertone. "Ladies' Room. Window."

"Triple play to home," said Tetra. "I get you."

So they went, Tetra and Bel leading, Morgan at their heels, plucking at their sleeves whenever anyone on the street looked his way.

The former customer's recommendation of the Bird on a Barseat as the proper place for Morgan, Tetra decided, had obviously been meant as an insult. Tetra had never seen a more disreputable-looking dive, not even in her samplings of the Gilhoolie waterfronts.

The door was narrow and flimsy, a cheap hollow-core plywood deal with no glass in it. The plate-glass windows with the place's name and logo painted on them, which flanked the door, were veined with cracks and the silvery tape used to repair them, and dirty to opacity.

Bel pushed open the door and stepped onto a floor of discolored black and white linoleum squares, some peeling up at the edges, some missing and displaying the stained cement beneath. A bar, the edge scalloped with burns and gouges, ran along the left-hand wall. Booths, the benches and tables of them similarly detailed, lined the wall to their right. No more than four feet of filthy floor separated the two features.

A mirror ran the length of the room behind the bar. It was a disturbing mirror, reflecting twice; a fainter image a quarter-inch to the side of the clear one. Other figures seemed to be reflected, too; shadowy figures whose originals couldn't be seen in the bar itself. A haunted mirror.

"Let us sit at a booth," Tetra suggested.

They did so, Bel and Tetra on one bench and Morgan on the other.

"Whatdayawant?" The bartender was tall and very thin; pale cream in color, with short spiky hair like dandelion seeds.

Tetra smiled at him, hoping he would show his teeth. He looked to her like something that would turn to dust if the sun ever hit it.

"Whatday a*want?*" He didn't alter his expression of indifference on the verge of hostility.

"Let us order something high in alcoholic content," said Tetra. "I would not trust him to wash a glass."

"I wouldn't trust him to slop a hog," said Morgan.

"Three straight anythings," said Bel, who didn't intend to stick around long enough to contract any diseases.

Morgan leaned across the table. "Dear girl," he began, and embarked upon a nearly operatic plea for mercy. He widened his cerulean eyes and smoothed his mustache. He put enough honey in his voice to send a cinnamon bear into a diabetic coma.

Bel admired the performance. She'd never seen a better one, not in eight years of teaching. *Oh, for a violin!* She almost wished she had the power Morgan thought she had, just so she could waive it.

A shadow fell across the table. A broad shadow; much too broad to belong to the etiolated bartender.

Slowly, with a sense of doom, Morgan and the women raised their heads.

District Criminal Investigator Pel Darzin stood before them, Officers Patth and Maeek at his sides, blocking any escape from the booth.

"We meet again," Darzin said to Tetra. "You shouldn't have run off, you know."

"We were chasing him," said Bel, with a jerk of her head toward Morgan. "We couldn't chase him if we didn't run off."

Darzin glanced from Tetra to Bel and back to Tetra. "Is this. . . ?"

Tetra nodded.

Darzin extended a thumb. "Bel," he said. "At last. I'm looking forward to your turn in court."

"How?" Morgan's head swiveled between Darzin and Bel and back again, like an unlatched gate in a gusty wind. "How?"

Darzin laughed. "Do you mean you didn't know? You didn't come here on purpose to give yourself up?"

Morgan goggled in reply.

Darzin stepped aside and raised a hand. The bartender pressed something under the bar, and the mirror dissolved, revealing the bustling observation post behind it. Darzin nodded, and the mirror returned.

Darzin beamed at Bel. "You knew, didn't you?"

"The Bird on a Barseat," she said. "Translation from the Earthling American English?"

"I believe so."

"The Stool Pigeon," said Tetra. "This planet takes some getting used to."

"I have a feeling we'll have plenty of time for it," said Bel.

"It's a trap?" Morgan's question was more of a statement.

"In your case, apparently, yes. In essence, no. You see the door in the back? Well, this place is in the rear of the Municipal Building. The Station House Headquarters, the General Council and Grand Council Chambers, the courtrooms. All through there."

"It's a trap," said Morgan. This time, it was definitely a statement.

"It's a convenience," said Darzin. "It makes things nice for our informers."

"Nice?" Bel, pulled her arm off the table with a sound like parting Velcro.

"Talk to the Appropriations Committee," said Darzin. "They must think this place pays for itself."

"Informers," said Morgan. "Informers like Ernie Foy, Jr., I suppose?"

"The man in the greasy hat?"

Morgan nodded.

"He's a new one," said Darzin. "We lost him for a while, but we'll have him back in time for the trial."

"The trial?" Bel shifted uncomfortably and thought about bail, posting and jumping. "When's the trial?"

"We can start just as soon as we get to the courtroom," said the DCI, "and add more charges as the witnesses arrive."

"I want a lawyer," said Morgan.

"What's a lawyer?"

Chapter 28

The time passed quickly for Freldt Saymak. After she recovered from being Mutt-and-Jeffed by the Gilhoolie siblings, she finished watching *Bambi.* She drew Batista into a discussion of the film's underlying thematic concepts, and learned, with dismay, that animals on Earth didn't really speak in vocal human language.

She listed the species of Llannonninn animals able to communicate in both Llannonninn and Allesesperanto: kronks, pays, schurr, dormin, and mantipil.

Then Batista told Freldt about dolphins and gorillas, and gorillas, as did most subjects, led him to poker.

He just happened to have a deck of cards with him. "Care to learn? Antonioni told me the rules. I understand some people play it regularly. Antonioni told me sometimes they even bet on the outcome."

"You mean, like money?" Freldt pulled a handful of eents, bihts, lumps and krelps from Bel's pocket.

"Uh, yeah. Tell you what: Let's just play for fun while you're learning. It'll be good practice for me, in case I ever get into one of those regular games."

Freldt rubbed a couple of coins together uncertainly. "If you think so," she said. "But I wouldn't want you to get used to doing it wrong, just because of me."

"Let's start out playing for markers," said Batista, his face reminiscent of the title character in the show Freldt had just watched. "Maybe after a while we'll play for your money against my credits. Just to make it more interesting."

"What are markers?"

"Something you use to stand for money, I think," said Batista. "We can use. . . ." He rummaged in the cabinets and brought out a box of individually wrapped tongue depressors. "These'll do."

"Explain it slowly," said Freldt.

"I'll have to. I know so little about the game! I think they call what I'm doing now 'dealing.'"

"You couldn't know less than I do. Have you ever noticed the numerals in the corners are the same as the number of diamonds and so on in the centers?"

~*~

When the door opened, Freldt, under the misapprehension Quatro had returned, threw herself to the floor and attempted to wriggle under the bed.

The Captain and Dr. Frazni observed silently for a moment, then Jinx spoke. "Have you lost something?"

Batista regarded Freldt sourly. "Has *she* lost something?"

Freldt stood and brushed herself off. "Uh," she said. "I found it."

Jinx dismissed Batista, who pocketed his cards and nothing else.

"You're very pleased with yourself," said Frazni.

"I enjoy making new friends."

"I hope you think of all of us as your friends," said Jinx. "Perhaps you don't remember me."

"I do. I owe you an apology: I'm sorry I made a scene, but I was frightened."

"We understand," said Frazni. "Please, don't apologize. We should apologize to you. It seems you've been seriously inconvenienced, at best."

"Oh, no," said Freldt. "I've been rescued. I have that to thank you for, too. Do you know who was responsible? Who gave the order to bring me aboard, I mean?"

"I did," said Jinx. "Captain Joan A. Fazzaria." She extended her hand, and Freldt hooked thumbs with her.

"I'm very pleased to meet you, Captain Joan A. Fazzaria. Is Operative Bel Schuster all right? Has Stokk Gord Pron been arrested? When can I go back to Llannonn?"

Jinx looked to Frazni, who said, "Go ahead, Captain. Be as candid as you like. She won't remember anything you don't want her to remember."

"Oh, absolutely," said Freldt. "I'm good at keeping secrets. Ask anybody."

"Operative Bel Schuster," said Jinx. "Stokk Gord Pron. It's a long story."

"When can I go home?"

"That's another long story."

"You can tell her—"

"I don't want to tell her, Dr. Frazni!"

The Bhat suppressed a smile. He had been reasonably certain the Captain would shy away from ordering him to wipe their captive's memory once she had met the woman. Being right never grew old.

"Ven Saymak," said the Captain, "we can't send you home, just yet. When we do, we could be in a lot of trouble for bringing you aboard without your permission."

"Oh, but I gave permission. In a way."

"You did?"

"Yes. Galactic Union Citizen Tetra Petrie, the small one, you know. . . ."

"I know."

"She told me to come with her, there in the lobby at Jok'rel's. And I came. Then, when the Galactic Union Space Trooper told me Operative Bel Schuster was round the bend, I said I looked forward to meeting her again. Then he said something, and I didn't understand what he said, and then. . . ."

"Then you transferred," said Frazni.

"Is that what we did? I didn't know, you see. We don't have transferring on Llannonn. Then I panicked. But, if I had understood what the Galactic Union Space Trooper said, and

I had known about transferring off Llannonn to the safety of a
Galactic Union ship, I would have agreed. He probably thought
I had. Everybody seemed to be in sort of a hurry."

"You don't consider yourself as having been taken and
held against your will?"

"Goodness, no," said the Bookkeeper. "Of course, the
Grand Council might think so, and take action in its own name.
Always possible, especially with Councilor Bella Yozgat on
the Board of Directors of the Llannonn for the Llannonninn
Movement, and the other Grand Councilor working with the
Stokk."

Jinx had her doubts about Bella Yozgat's motives. *Is the
traitor another Grand Councilor, or the same?*

"Exactly," she said. "But, assuming we could get you back
on planet without anyone knowing you had left, you wouldn't
feel compelled to complain of us?"

"For cooperating with the police?" Freldt laughed merrily.
"What an absurd idea!"

"Isn't it?" The Captain laughed, too, in as close a
counterfeit to merriment as she could manage. "But suppose
— just suppose, mind you — someone told you we *haven't*
been cooperating with the police."

"Oh, that would be very different." Freldt thought a
moment. "A different thing entirely. —*Are* you telling me?"

Jinx's mouth formed the word No. She cleared her throat.
"No," she said, "I'm not telling you that. I just wondered."

Freldt smiled again.

"Then," said Jinx, "suppose someone told you it's
absolutely vital to the future of successful cooperation between
the Galactic Union and Llannonn that you never volunteer a
word about any of this. Not even to the police or the Grand
Council."

"Then I'd never say a word. Not a word. I'd pretend to
myself I went home when I left the Inn and took a nice long
nap and then came back for the evening floor show."

"Good! Good story! I like it!"

"*Are* you telling me it's vital—"

"Yes! Absolutely vital!"

Jinx and Freldt hooked thumbs again.

"We'll return you to the Inn very soon," said the Captain.

"Will I ever see Operative Bel Schuster again?"

Will any of us ever see Operative Bel Schuster again? "I doubt it," she said.

~*~

As they approached the transfer alcove, Jinx snapped, "Wipe that self-satisfied smirk off your face, Doctor, or I'll have you up on charges."

Vlador Frazni laughed aloud.

Jinx wouldn't have been surprised if the alcove had been out of order, but it wasn't. She took it as an encouraging sign. She needed to.

"Do you think we can trust her?"

"Unquestionably," said the Empathetic Diagnostician. "She won't say a word. As long as she isn't asked."

By a convenience of physics, it was purely a fiction of the horror genre that transfer subjects could become interparticulated with any other object. If a someone or something transferred to a spot occupied by another someone or something, the someone or something being transferred would, like a playing piece on a game board, be bumped to the next available space.

So Jinx found herself saying, "You had to say that, didn't you?" into Quatro Petrie's left shoulder blade, rather than Dr. Frazni's right ear.

"I beg your pardon, Captain," said Quatro. "Are you speaking to me?"

"No," said Captain Fazzaria. "Never mind. Did we miss anything?"

"Just Petrie," said Hessaphess, "telling us how to do our jobs."

"Not how to do your jobs," said Quatro. "I would never presume to do so. How to do them more efficiently."

"So sorry," said Hessaphess, with the leaden sarcasm for which he was so widely known. "I must have misunderstood."

"Quite all right," said Quatro. "It isn't the first time, and it won't be the last."

"If we could all be seated. . . ," said the Captain. "Now. Our time is nearly up. I believe we're agreed the only thing we can do at this point is to persuade the Stokk to take Ven Schuster back to Jok'rel's Inn."

"Actually," said Quatro, "that isn't the only thing we can do. It's merely the most legitimate."

"You have another suggestion, Ven Petrie?"

"We have Professor Schuster's coordinates. We have her scan pattern. It would be illegal, but not difficult, to transfer her from where she is now. This is a starship. Perhaps I'm not *too* foolish in assuming the engines are in proper working order."

"Sit down, Wotan," said Captain Fazzaria.

"We could be out of orbit and halfway out of the Sector before anyone down there knew what was happening."

"And how would we explain it to the Llannonninn government? Or to ours?"

Quatro leaned back in his chair and spread his hands. "We blame it all on Professor Schuster."

"Blaming it all on Professor Schuster seems rather unkind," Jinx began.

"It *is* all her fault," said Hessaphess.

"But it hardly seems sportsmanlike," said Jinx.

"I think it'll fit," said Chestney.

"Well," said Jinx.

"Let's not count our plots before they're hatched," said the Doctor. "The poor woman——"

"Captain!" The voice of Donna Meichi made them all jump. "I have another call from Llannonn."

"Same location as before?"

"No, Captain."

I knew things were looking too bright. They've moved her.

"Can you lock on?"

"I don't need to, Captain. It's from a courtroom in the Council City Municipal Building. From District Criminal Investigator Pel Darzin."

Chapter 29

"District Criminal Investigator?"

"Yes, Captain. Of the Meadow of Flowers District, to be exact."

"Meadow of Flowers?"

Chestney worked some keys. "The District of which Council City is also the Central City," he said.

"Put him through, Ven Meichi."

A hologram appeared across the desk from the Crisis Team; the image of a short, almost pudgy man with high rounded cheekbones, black hair, skin the color of vanilla wafers, and large brown eyes with long thick eyelashes.

"Have I the honor of addressing Captain Joan A. Fazzaria of the Galactic Union Ship *St. Gregory the Wonderworker?*"

"Yes. District Criminal Investigator Pel Darzin?"

"Yes." The DCI beamed. "I can't tell you how pleased I am to speak to you face — well, almost face-to-face. It's been quite a day, Captain Joan A. Fazzaria."

"It has, indeed, District Criminal Investigator Pel Darzin."

"I've been given the honor," said Darzin, "of expressing the thanks of the people of Llannonn for your prompt and effective work in the apprehension of the Criminal Connell Morgan."

WHO? "You're, uh, quite welcome."

"I have also the honor of asking you and any guests you might care to bring to descend to this location to receive the personal and official thanks of the Grand Council—" he paused for breath— "which will be given directly after the trial."

I knew it.

"The trial? Whose trial?"

"Everybody's trial. Please say you'll come."

"Uh. . . . When you say, 'Everybody's,' do you mean. . . . I mean, is there anybody I know?"

"Oh, yes." Darzin laughed. "I should say there is."

"In that case," said Fazzaria, "I will, naturally, attend."

"Good. Good. I have one final happy message to deliver: The Grand Council appreciates your delicacy in removing your personnel from Llannonn, but your assistance in bringing the Criminal Connell Morgan to justice exonerates you from the shame of his crimes. Your people are most welcome to return, and the Grand Council will immediately petition the Galactic Union Ambassador for closer ties."

Jinx sat stunned under this barrage of goodwill. "I'm so pleased," she managed to say.

Chestney whispered something, but she didn't hear it. He repeated his question in a stage whisper so loud the communications amplifier picked it up. "When is the trial?"

"It's taking place right now. You've already missed the Stokk, I'm afraid, but if you hurry, you'll be in time for the rest of it. You say you will attend?"

"Did I? I mean, yes, thank you, District Criminal Investigator Pel Darzin. Just mark the courtroom on the Council's transfer map with the attached locator pen."

"Yes, I've done it."

"We'll be right there."

"I'll inform the Archon. She won't mind waiting a bit. See you soon."

"Thank you. Um. Thank you."

Darzin terminated contact.

Jinx looked at her advisors. Quatro cleared his throat, but said nothing.

"No mention of Schuster," said Wotan Hessaphess.

"No word from or of Tetra," said Quatro.

"But he said the trial included someone we know."

"He also," Quatro said, "seemed to, if I may be permitted use of the word, *assume* we know this Criminal Connell Morgan; are, in fact, connected to him in some way, and are somehow responsible for his capture."

"Yes, Quatro," said the Captain. "I know he did. I was here, remember?"

"My point," Quatro said, with great dignity, "is that perhaps the District Criminal Investigator has got hold of the wrong end of the stick, or of some stick totally unconnected with Professor Schuster. Perhaps the Stokk of which he spoke are different Stokk altogether. Perhaps we may still hear from the Stokk holding the professor."

"Perhaps," said Jinx, "we might as well admit we don't have the foggiest notion of what the black hole is going on. Shore leave will continue to be rescinded until I've made sure this isn't some sort of trap. I'll transfer immediately."

Chestney objected, "But, Captain, if it's a trap, is it wise for you to transfer down? Shouldn't we send someone expendable?"

Quatro and Hessaphess eyed each other.

Jinx ignored it all. "Dr. Frazni, I'd like you to come with me, in case worse comes to worst and you're needed to testify to the well-being of our Llannonninn guest. Harry, return to the bridge and take the conn. Wotan — Professor Petrie — Thank you for your help."

"Captain," said Quatro. "Request permission to accompany you to Llannonn."

"Whatever for? It could be dangerous. We already seem to have misplaced two members of our teaching staff down there."

"One of whom is my only litter-mate," said Quatro. His failure to elaborate was eloquent.

"Permission granted."

Force of Habit

~*~

Fazzaria, Frazni, and Petrie arrived, not in the courtroom, but in a corridor floored in marble tiles and lined with polished wooden benches.

DCI Pel Darzin met them.

"Hello, hello," he said, extending his thumb to each of them in turn. "Glad you could make it. I thought it would be better if I greeted you out here; then we won't disrupt the court. I don't need a contempt charge added to my sheet."

"You're one of the everybody? I mean, you're on trial?"

"Oh, yes," said Darzin. "Quite right, too. The court's in a brief recess just now; we've been waiting for you."

Darzin reached for the door handle, but Captain Fazzaria stopped him with a hand on his arm.

"Ouch!"

"Sorry. Are. . . . Are *we* part of the everybody?"

"Are you on trial, you mean?" Darzin rubbed his arm. "No, not that I know of. Should you be?"

"No," said Jinx. "Ha, ha." Perhaps she should have taken Quatro's first advice; dumped the bookkeeper and made star tracks back when she'd had the chance.

Darzin reached for the latch again, shied, and, with an eye on the Captain, opened the door.

The courtroom looked like an auditorium designed by Oscar Wilde. There were ten sofas, four of them full of what turned out to be witnesses. Before each sofa stretched a glass-topped coffee table, the tables in front of the occupied sofas set with cups, spoons, teapots, creamers, sugar bowls, sugar tongs, bowls of lemon slices, and plates of small thin sandwiches.

Six wing chairs stood two-by-two under the far windows, a refreshment table between each two. In each pair of chairs sat a man and a woman. The Captain recognized Bella Yozgat and Thomms Nyakk in one pair, and deduced these six were the Grand Council of Llannonn, grouped by sociotype.

Jinx had no trouble pegging them. Yozgat and Nyakk, she knew, were Urbanites, but their sophisticated dress and polished manner would have told her so anyway.

In another pair of chairs sat a tall, rangy man with tanned, deeply lined skin and large hands; and a woman, nearly as tall, 250 pounds of what looked like pure muscle. Both wore trousers under tunics slung with sashes going from one shoulder to the opposite hip. Rurals.

The final pair had to be Wanderers: The man was of average height, and definitely plump. He wore a soft yellow shirt, much too tight for someone with so much fat where his muscle should be, rings on eight of his ten fingers and another in one ear. The woman wore a dress covered with ruffles and bows. Shopping bags sat on the floor next to her.

The Archon sat in a Morris chair in front of the Councilors, facing the courtroom. A table at her elbow bore a cup and a plate, both full. Printouts covered the table before her.

The Archon, herself, was tall, full, and solid. Her graying black hair snarled in an ineffectively brushed tangle beneath her orange beret of office. She wore a red and orange floral print blouse, black trousers, a black sweater-vest, black sandals, and an electric blue chiffon neckerchief. No one could deny the power of her appearance.

As Darzin led the Unionites into the room, the Archon raised eyes as electrically blue as her scarf and spoke, with deliberate enthusiasm, in a voice calculated to override any competitive vocalizations. "Ah, Captain, and party. So glad you could join us. District Criminal Investigator Pel Darzin, I believe you are one of the accused?"

"Yes, Mercy."

"Please join the others until you're called."

"Yes, Mercy." Darzin waved goodbye to the GU group and left the courtroom.

"Please be seated," said the Archon. "Usher, help them

to a seat and get them some tea and sandwiches. No telling how long this may take. I'm just looking over the documents, here."

There was a murmur of talk while the Usher led the Captain, the Doctor, and the Professor to a couch and served them. Then the Archon fixed Jinx with her blue steel eye again. "Have you been told about the Stokk?"

"No," said Jinx. "Well, told about, no. No, I haven't."

"We've just finished with them. It didn't take long. Couple of kidnappers. Arrested in a joint effort by the Police Force and the Communications Commission. Nice piece of work. Cooperation between law enforcement branches, and so on. They confessed immediately, and apologized, both of which helped their positions immensely, of course. Blamed everything on their employer, which is usually the way it is with Stokk. No surprises, there, eh?"

She leaned over one arm of her chair to collect the smiles and nods of the Grand Council. "They gave us one surprise, though, didn't they?" The Council stopped smiling and gave one another dirty looks.

The Archon turned around again. "They claimed we have a renegade in our midst," she explained to the Captain. "They say one of the Grand Council is offering to work with them. Conspiracy to commit crimes and misdemeanors in opposition to the laws of the free market and in breach of etiquette. What do you think of that?"

"I'm shocked. Shocked," said Jinx.

The Archon nodded. "Shocked," she said. "Well, so was I. Yes, yes, so was I. So. Was. I. Did you want to say something?"

"I just. . . . I just wonder. . . . What happened to her . . . them . . . who. . . ."

The Archon waited a patient moment, then said, "I'm not sure I follow you, Captain Joan A. Fazzaria."

Jinx attempted a smile, and wished she'd left it out. "You said they were a couple of kidnappers. The person . . . people . . . whoever they kidnapped. I just wondered what happened to her . . . them."

"Yes, I see what you mean, now. Naturally, you'd be concerned. We'll be coming to that, directly."

"Oh," said Jinx, weakly. "Good."

Quatro whispered into Jinx's ear. "Still no names. It could mean Ven Schuster is still undetected. She could have escaped during the arrest and made her way back to the Inn. Once there, Tetra would have seen to it she remained undetected until she could be transferred back aboard under the cover of Tetra's return."

Captain Fazzaria crumbled a sugar cube into her tea. "Do you really think so?"

Dr. Frazni touched a pressure point on the Captain's head, and the twitch in her cheek subsided.

The Archon returned to her printouts, making an occasional notation, and brushing at the sandwich crumbs which fell upon them. After five of the longest minutes of Jinx's life, the Archon scanned the room until she found the Usher.

"Court is resumed," she said.

"Court is resumed, everybody!" The Usher stuck his head into the hall and Jinx heard his voice calling, "Court, everybody!" He pulled his head back in. "Carry on," he said.

"Let's have the accused," said the Archon.

The Usher unlocked a panel on the wall near the door and flipped a switch.

The wall to the court's right, actually a combination of hologram and sound-baffle, dissolved.

Six padded chairdesks appeared behind where the false wall had been, a prisoner fettered to each chair with long chains cuffed around both ankles and both wrists. Each desk was supplied with a cup of tea and a selection of sandwiches.

To denote the prisoners' status as defendants, the crusts of their sandwiches had not been cut off.

Three of the prisoners, one of them with very large feet and wearing a blue tunic, were strangers to the Captain. The third prisoner was Pel Darzin. The others were Professor Bel Schuster and Professor Tetra Petrie.

Chapter 30

"Now, then," said the Archon. "Who shall we have up next?"

One of the witnesses rose. "If you please, Mercy," he said, "most of us are here to testify against Galactic Union Citizen Connell Morgan." The other witnesses grumbled agreement. "If we could do him first, those of us who want to could go on home."

"Point well taken," said the Archon. "Galactic Union Citizen Connell Morgan it is, then. Will the Sergeant at Arms please bring the prisoner forward?"

The Sergeant at Arms was an older woman, very thin. She wore sensible black shoes and a dress of the same red-and-orange floral print as the Archon's blouse. From the left side of her black belt dangled a ring of keys; from the right, a sack of disposable dampened towels. She had a metal thimble fixed to the middle finger of each hand.

At the Archon's order, the Sergeant pressed a foot pedal on the back of the blue-tunic man's chairdesk. With a faint mechanical hum, wheels extruded from each leg of the chair.

Morgan grabbed at his refreshments as the Sergeant wheeled him to face the witnesses and pressed the pedal again, lowering him into place.

"I didn't spill your tea, did I?"

Morgan licked his fingers. "Much you care," he said.

"Oh, now," said the Sergeant. She pulled a towel from her sack and wiped Morgan's face and hands.

"I can do it," he said.

"Of course you can." She gave him the towel and took up a post just behind him and to his left.

"Galactic Union Citizen Connell Morgan," the Archon said, reading from one of her printout sheets, "it says here you are accused, in the name of the laws of Llannonn, of fraud, among other things. What do you have to say for yourself?"

"Where I come from," said Morgan, "an alleged criminal is charged with a specific crime and defends himself (or herself, as the case may be) from that specific charge."

"Are you from Llannonn?"

"No, of course not."

"Then this isn't where you come from. And that isn't the way we do things here. Do you have anything to say for yourself before we start hearing witnesses?"

"I can't say anything unless I know exactly what I'm charged with, can I?"

"Oh, I think you could, if you had a mind to." The Archon fixed Morgan with her gimlet stare until his own blue eyes, defenseless before hers, shifted.

The Archon nodded to the Usher, who said, "First Witness."

One of the witnesses, a man, stood.

"State your name," said the Usher.

"Real Estate Agent Heathcliff Brontay."

"Begin witness."

"The accused," Heathcliff Brontay said, "presented himself to me as an authorized representative of the Earthling Historical Monument and Realty Agency, Deep Space Franchise. Knowing the Grand Council had approved shore leave for the Galactic Union ship *St. Gregory the Wonderworker,* I invested heavily in the goods offered by the accused. Have you seen his brochure?" He reached into the pocket of his jacket, but the Archon waved a slick pamphlet at him.

"Very appealing," said the Archon.

"But then," said Brontay, "when I approached the Earthlings with my merchandise, thinking to give them the chance to ease their homesickness, to provide them with ownership of meaningful and desirable pieces of their home planet—"

"Grant's Tomb," said another witness.

"The Kremlin," said another.

"Choice building lots on Atlantis—" Brontay tried to continue.

A female from one of the other sofas rose. "Mount Rushmore," she said. "I paid a pretty krelp for that one, I can tell you."

The Archon tapped a sugar spoon against the side of her teacup to bring the woman to order. "Your name?"

"Bathsheba Squeers, Mercy."

"Well, wait your turn, Bathsheba Squeers."

"Yes, Mercy."

"Continue, Real Estate Agent Heathcliff Brontay."

"The Earthlings laughed at me. Ridiculed me. Called me a 'con artist.' Offered to buy me a drink and asked my price for the Brooklyn Bridge, as if it were a joke."

Bathsheba Squeers rose again, her mouth open, her finger pointing to herself.

"Wait your turn," said the Archon, quellingly, and the complainant sat back, distracting her neighbors with her mumbles.

One by one, the witnesses against Morgan stood and repeated approximately the same story. One of them was Squanto Uncas, the man who had briefly shared Tetra's table, offering to sell her, she now remembered, "genuine Earthling real estate."

When all the witnesses against Morgan had been heard, the Archon said, "Captain Joan A. Fazzaria!"

Jinx's cup rattled, slopping a pool of tea into the saucer. "Yes, er, Mercy?"

"What can you tell us about this?"

"I never saw him before in my life," said Jinx. "Never

heard of him until District Criminal Investigator Pel Darzin mentioned him earlier."

"Be that as it may. Why did your crewmembers laugh at these honest businessfolk?"

The witnesses twisted around to regard her over the backs of their sofas.

"Well," said Jinx. "Most of the 'items' I've heard about today are public property, some of them are defunct if not imaginary, and the rest are privately owned by people I seriously doubt are selling, certainly not through him."

"I suspected as much. It's clearly fraud, then, isn't it? Is that specific enough for you, Galactic Union Citizen Connell Morgan?"

"But wait!" said the Usher. "There's more!"

The Archon tapped her printouts with an imperious finger. "Why do I not have notice of it?"

"It's a surprise witness," said the Usher. "Surprise!"

The Archon bobbed her head and lifted her hands in the universal gesture for *Very well, then, let's have it.*

The Usher strode to the courtroom doors, announcing, as he strode, "Gentlebeings, I present to you —" he threw the doors wide, "Assistant Librarian Holly Jahangiri!"

Sensation in the court.

Jinx failed to see the reason for the sensation, unless it was the almost otherworldly fluffiness of the purple feather boa around the woman's neck. Apparently, though, it was her profession rather than her person which caused the stir, for witnesses turned to one another with murmurs of *Who?* and *Which library?* and *Gosh!*

The Assistant Librarian approached the Mercy table and Council bench, bowed to the officials, and turned to face the courtroom.

"District Criminal Investigator Pel Darzin," — She and the DCI exchanged warm, shy glances — "contacted me some weeks ago about a new businessman in town. It seems a man had been selling Earth names, and the DCI hoped I could help the police determine whether or not this man had the proper license to do so. I regretted to inform him — for who among us doesn't regret dishonesty? — that names on Earth, like those on Llannonn, *require no license to use and are free for the taking*."

Another sensation. The Usher and the Sergeant at Arms set forth a disharmonious two-toned growl that set Jinx's teeth on edge.

The Archon bowed the court's gratitude to the Assistant Librarian and motioned her to the softest of the witness couches.

"Here, now," said Morgan. "Are you going to let her just walk in and start saying things? Aren't you going to make her swear to tell the truth or something?"

"Make her swear to tell the truth?" the Archon said, over the hubbub. "She's a *librarian!*"

Cries of *paid a premium, two for the price of one special deal*, and *money-back guarantee* flew about the courtroom until the Archon was forced to rap on the table with knuckles like tempered brass.

Morgan had sat through the witnesses' tirades, a model of dignity and decorum. Now he used his dampened towel to dab at the corners of his mouth.

"I'm afraid," he said, sorrow thickening his warm Irish voice like honey in a toddy, "it is all too true. All too sadly true."

The witnesses sat back in various attitudes of anticipated satisfaction.

Morgan spread his manacled hands wide and, sweeping the couches with a look that would melt the nose of a Communications Commission Official, said, "I apologize. I have brought shame to myself, shame to my people, shame to my friends. I beg you: Forgive me." He bent his head and covered his face with his hands, being sure to shake just enough to jingle his chains.

"Very pretty," said the Archon.

One of the witnesses sobbed aloud. Several sniffed, and several others offered them handkerchiefs. After a moment of unbridled nose-blowing, the court returned to order.

"Galactic Union Citizen Connell Morgan," the Archon declared, "you are obviously guilty, and liable to pay the full penalty of the law."

Morgan's head snapped up so suddenly it made the Sergeant jump. "What? I apologized, didn't I?"

"Yes," said the Archon. "And you did it very nicely, too. Brief, but well phrased, and very much to the point. Still, there are times when a simple, 'I'm sorry,' just isn't enough, wouldn't you say?"

"What more do you want from me?"

"Criminal justice is a house with three rooms," said the Archon, steepling her fingers. "Sometimes one must go through all three of the rooms in order to leave the house. The names of the rooms are Remorse, Atonement, and Recompense."

There was a scattering of applause.

"You've shown proper remorse," the Archon's tone and choice of emphasis seemed to underline the distinction between showing and feeling, "but what about the rest of it?"

"What about it?"

"I just wondered if you had any suggestions to offer."

"I suggest you deport me immediately. It would teach me a lesson I'd never forget."

"No doubt. No doubt. But it still ignores the question of recompense. How are you going to repay these fine people for the trouble and money you've cost them? Not to mention court costs and assorted intangible damages?"

"I can't," said Morgan. "The money's spent. It's gone, I tell you. I don't have two credits to bless myself with."

"How unfortunate for you," said the Archon. "Fraud, and other charges we haven't mentioned as yet, and you have no meaningful atonement or restitution to offer— You leave me no choice but to inflict the severest possible penalty the law allows. You won't like it. I think I ought to warn you, well in advance, that you won't like it."

Morgan twisted his dampened towel until moisture dripped from it. "No. Please. I'll get the money. Captain! Somebody! Please!"

"I wasn't finished," said the Archon.

"But you can't do this!"

The Sergeant at Arms rapped Morgan on the head with her right-hand thimble.

"Ouch!"

The Sergeant folded her arms across her chest as if daring the prisoner to protest the just and righteous thump.

"As I say, I wasn't finished. Now, where was I? Oh, yes. Now we come to the matter of kidnapping, holding for ransom, and illegal use of a communications device."

"I thought that was the Stokk," Jinx whispered to Quatro. "Wasn't that the Stokk?"

Quatro lifted his shoulders and shook his head. "I suppose we'll find out."

"I suppose anything's possible," said Jinx.

"You want to talk to *her* about that," said Morgan, pointing to Bel at the full extent his chain would allow. "That's *her* fault, all of it. Talk about fraud. What's your real name, then? Brigid O'Shaughnessy?"

Bel looked at her fellow prisoners, then at the empty space on her other side. "Are you talking to me?"

Morgan took several steps toward her, dragging his chair by the chains, before the Sergeant grabbed his ear and gave it what looked like quite a painful twist.

He resumed his seat.

"Now," said the Sergeant, "are you going to sit quietly, and mind your manners?"

"Yes! I'll be good! I promise!"

The Sergeant released the prisoner's ear. "I'll believe it when I see it," she said.

The Archon made some notes. "I'm adding on the cost of the crockery you've just smashed. I would be extremely careful, if I were you. Your punishment couldn't get much worse, but nothing's ever as bad as it might be, now is it?"

Morgan said nothing. The Archon looked up, obviously expecting an answer.

"Whatever you say, Mercy," said Connell.

"Nicely put," said the Archon. She turned her attention to Bel. "Is your name Brigid O'Shaughnessy?"

"No, Mercy. It's Professor Isobel Enid Schuster of the Galactic Union."

Jinx bit a nail. *Sounds like an action/adventure show. "Professor Isobel Enid Schuster of the Galactic Union. Fighting criminal ignorance across the galaxy."*

"And is Galactic Union Citizen Connell Morgan's guilt in these latter charges all your fault? Are you guilty of fraud?"

Say no. Jinx tried to project the words across the room. She crossed her fingers. She crossed her toes. She crossed her eyes. *Say no.*

"Yes," said Bel. "I'm afraid I am. I misled the accused Galactic Union Citizen Connell Morgan. I deceived him. I outright lied to him. I persuaded him to make an unauthorized call on my squawkbox to my ship, which was under a communications interdiction. I did the very same thing to the Stokk, in the case just before this one. They didn't complain, and I didn't want to interrupt."

"Commendable," said the Archon. "So you confess, do you?"

"No," said Jinx.

"Yes," said Bel.

"In that case, Galactic Union Citizen Connell Morgan, the court chooses to substitute a lesser penalty."

The witnesses muttered protests, which the Archon squelched with a comprehensive glance.

"I hereby sentence you to be sold to the Meadow of Flowers Wandering Tribe. Your price, as well as most of your earnings, will go as financial restitution to your victims. Then you can start earning your freedom."

"That's the *revised* sentence?"

"Yes. And you have this noble woman to thank for it."

"What was the sentence before you revised it?"

"You were going to be skinned alive and drawn through town in a barrel studded with sharp nails, pulled by a chemically maddened pratty. If you'd broken any more of my good dishes, we'd have put hot sauce on the nails."

Morgan got his eyes back in focus. "Thank you," he said to Bel. He sounded as if he meant it.

"Any more charges against this man? No? That's done for you, then," said the Archon. "Let's do Bel Schuster next."

Chapter 31

Jinx pictured herself, Frazni, and Quatro fighting their way to Schuster's and Petrie's sides, calling for a transfer, and getting the hell out of Dodge.

Bel, seeing the Captain's coffee-bean complexion turn to the color of milk with a dash of prune juice, pictured the senior Officer swooning in court.

"It's all right, Captain," she said, more in hope than in certainty, as the Sergeant rolled her into place. "Honest people have nothing to fear in an honest court."

The witnesses cheered.

"Well said," said the Archon. "Well said. Do you have anything else to say, before we call witnesses?"

"Don't forget the other one," said Morgan. "The little one. She's as bad as Schuster. They're in it together, passing secret messages and codes and so on. Thought you put those past me, didn't you?"

"We did put them past you," said Tetra.

"You did? I mean, you did not."

The Archon addressed Tetra. "Name?"

"Professor Tetra Petrie of the Galactic Union."

"Together with her trusty sidekick. . . ," Jinx wandered.

"Is what he says true? *Are* you Professor Isobel Enid Schuster's partner in her crimes?"

"I am," said Tetra. "And proud of the partnership, though repentant of the crimes."

"That goes double for me," said Bel. She felt an unaccustomed prickle behind her eyes.

The witnesses cheered again.

213

"I like your attitude," said the Archon. "We rarely see off-worlders with such proper moral comprehension, if I may so express myself. One wonders how the two of you ever came to break the law in the first place."

"Yes," Jinx breathed. "Doesn't one?"

Darzin smiled to himself. It was all so simple. He wasn't surprised no one else had pieced it together; no one else had all the fragments. No one else had been as deeply involved with all the events, from beginning to end, as he had been. No doubt the Captain knew some of it; so did Darlla Bute; so did the Good Citizen Wandering Tribeswoman who, Darzin had noted with a shock, was actually a member of the Grand Council. But none of these had the whole story. It was possible, he thought, not even the agents knew as much about what had happened as he did.

Darzin stood in his chains. "If I may be permitted to speak, Mercy. . . ."

"Go right ahead."

"I believe I can answer your questions, though these women and I only met briefly."

"Then please do."

"We know of the crimes of Galactic Union Citizen Connell Morgan."

"We certainly do," said Bathsheba Squeers, dissatisfied buyer of the Brooklyn Bridge.

"Can we assume he only became a criminal on Llannonn? I think not. He was a criminal before he ever fouled our planet. And the Galactic Union knew it."

"And they let him come," said Bella Yozgat. "Nice of them, wasn't it?"

"They had no proof," said Darzin. "They had no witnesses. Otherwise, they would have dealt with him before he inflicted himself on us. But they didn't simply let him come. No. They followed him. They followed him, in the person of their agent."

"A spy, in effect!" Councilor Yozgat just wasn't going to give it up.

"A spy comes in disguise," said Darzin. "The Galactic Union agent came as exactly what she is: a professor on a Galactic Union teaching ship."

Everyone looked at the professors.

The professors looked at each other and spoke in chorus: "You're a spy?"

"Is it only coincidence the Galactic Union signed a contract with Jok'rel's Traveler's Rest Inn, one of the haunts of the criminal?"

"According to my information," said the Archon, tapping her printouts, "he haunts a lot of places. In fact, it would have taken the Galactic Union years of research to find a low-to-moderately priced place he *didn't* haunt."

"True, Mercy, but that's the elegance of all this: No one part of it seems related to any other part. But, taking all the parts together, the whole truth is both simple and obvious."

"Continue."

"So, the agent came to the Inn certain that, sometime during her leave, she would be approached by the criminal Connell Morgan or one of his victims. Then she would have her proof. But then, something happened."

Darzin put his hands behind his back and attempted to pace; a difficult feat, when chained to a desk.

"The agent fell into conversation with one of us. It may have been chance, or the agent's trained powers of observation may have called her to the aid of someone in the most desperate danger. For there was such a person at the Inn; Bookkeeper Freldt Saymak."

A murmur ran around the courtroom.

"Yes," said Darzin. "You've heard the name before. The Stokk confessed their designs on her, didn't they? But they were in such a rush to throw the blame on others, they didn't make it clear they never had her, did they? But they made it clear to me, when I arrested them in the criminal Connell Morgan's lair. They didn't have her because the agent changed clothes with her."

Bel looked down at the lilac double-breasted jumpsuit with the plaid peplum which she still wore, and she cursed it silently but heartily.

Darzin leaned his knuckles on his desk and said, "The agent I came to know as 'Bel' deliberately put herself in danger of the criminals and of the law. She deliberately led both the Stokk Gord Pron and Galactic Union Citizen Connell Morgan away from the Inn and deliberately absorbed both their attacks. She deliberately broke communications interdiction with her ship, knowing she would thereby draw attention to the kidnappers' location. She sent all manner of messages to Llannonn law enforcers, even though she knew, by assuring the capture and conviction of the criminals, she created the evidence assuring her own."

The Archon looked as puzzled as Jinx felt. "Why?"

"That's just the way I am," said Bel.

"Noble," whispered one of the Council.

"Her co-agent, as well," said Darzin, waving a clinking hand at Tetra, "knowingly broke the law in order to assist it. If it hadn't been for her crimes, our invasion of the culprits' den might have been ineffective at best and fatal to Galactic Union Agent Bel Schuster at worst. And so you see Galactic Union Co-agent Professor Tetra Petrie here in chains, as well."

"That is just the way I am, too," said Tetra.

"Captain Joan A. Fazzaria," said the Archon. "Can you prove the truth of any of this?"

Prove the truth of it? I didn't even follow it.

"Do you, for instance, know the location at which the agents were being held?"

"Oh, yes," said Jinx, happy to be asked a simple question for which she knew the simple answer. "We had the location."

"And didn't use it," said Darzin. "Because the Galactic Union never intended to interfere with Llannonninn justice, only to assist it, even if it meant the sacrifice of two of its top agents."

The Archon looked at Jinx, who said, weakly, "That's just the way we are."

"But what made anyone think," said the Archon, "Llannonninn justice needed assistance? Haven't we always been competent to handle our own affairs? Are we any less competent now? And, if so, why?"

Darzin darted a glance across the row of Grand Councilors and met the Archon's eye.

"I see what you mean," she said.

This matter of the false Councilor was one Bel had not had much leisure to consider. She considered it now, and found the conclusion inescapable. She knew who it was.

Who had accosted her when she had first left the Inn? Who had followed her? Who had sat, like a cat at a mousehole, until the Stokk had arrived? Who sat in court, now, looking innocent as a new-laid egg with a bow on it?

"There's your traitor," she said, pointing at the bag lady.

The bag lady's eyes and mouth popped open as she turned to her compatriot. "Councilor Kalator Ganev?"

The plump man in the tight yellow shirt snarled something at Bel. He snarled in Llannonninn, but it must have been juicy, because everybody blushed.

"How did you know? Even Councilor Resa Stelissto, here, didn't know. How did you find me out?"

Bel still pointed toward the Wandering Tribes representatives, her mouth still set in a triumphant smile, though her eyes were glazing over.

"That," said Tetra, "would be telling."

The Archon stuck her pencil behind her ear and sat back. "It seems to me," she said, "the motives and results of their crimes, coupled with the very proper remorse they've both shown, should absolve these women. I think we should dismiss all charges against them, don't you?"

The suggestion was approved by voice.

A howl arose from one of the sofas, and a grubby girl-child threw herself to the floor at Bel's feet.

"I'm sorry! I'm sorry!"

Darzin recognized the penitent. "Juvenile Genesis Selinsky! What's the matter?"

"I'm sorry!" The child lifted her body enough to extract and extend an object.

"My moneybelt!"

"Punish me! Sell me! Send me to bed without dessert!"

"Do we have a new case to add to the docket?" The Archon pulled her pencil from behind her ear.

"No," said Bel. "No case. No problem. No more time in court." She fastened her belt under her peplum. "See?"

"You're not pressing charges?"

"Against this precious child? I wouldn't dream of it."

Genesis Selinsky backed, bowing, to her sofa and sat next to Assistant Librarian Holly Jahangiri, her eyes aflame with devotion.

"Three cheers for the heroine!" Darzin led the acclamation. "Hip, hip—"

"Hip!" The crowd tossed their hats into the air, then milled around sorting them out and getting them back to their proper owners.

The Archon tapped her teacup until the delicate vessel was in danger of shattering. "We have yet before us the charges against *you*, District Criminal Investigator Pel Darzin and Police Officer Ander Patth. . . ." The Archon threw her spoon over her shoulder. "What the what. The court forgives them, as well. Any objections?"

Communications Commission Official Darlla Bute held up her charge sheet and tore it in two. There was yet another sensation in court.

"Councilor Kalator Ganev—"

"Mercy, I confess, and I repent." The guilty Councilor rent open his shirt, exposing much that would have been better left enshrouded. "I herewith abdicate my position on the Councils, General and Grand, and announce my retirement from politics. I will leave my beloved Council City, and exile myself to the outer District. I will sell myself to a country-based Tribe, and donate my price to the Committee for Purity in Government."

The Archon rapped the table with her knuckles. "Done! Sergeant Polly, release the Professors and the Officers."

Sergeant Polly did so, and the former prisoners mingled, hooking thumbs and trading introductions.

"Well, I think that just about takes care of everything, doesn't it?"

"Not quite everything," said Councilor Resa Stelissto. "I have some testimony of my own to give."

The Tribeswoman addressed the court. "I was out this afternoon, minding my own business," she touched the handles of one of her bags, "doing some shopping, when I got drawn into this." She nodded at Pel Darzin, who blushed manfully.

"I apologize for not recognizing you, Councilor," he said. "I pride myself on knowing all the Grand Councilors and some of the General Councilors on sight. I can't think why. . . ."

Resa Stelissto waved down his apology. "This is a new outfit, and I just had my hair done. You couldn't have been more courteous if you *had* recognized me; don't think another thing of it."

Darzin blushed more manfully than ever.

"At any rate," the Councilor continued, "While I stood watch for District Criminal Investigator Pel Darzin at Convict Connell Morgan's lair, this fell from a window." She drew a slip of paper from her bosom and read from it. "'Prisoner. Freldt Saymak. Police. Bel Schuster.' I was taking it to the police when I saw DCI Pel Darzin returning to the scene with a squad of

Officers. I was already late for an appointment, so I returned to work. You say this one—" she pointed to Bel, "is Bel Schuster. What I want to know is: Where's Freldt Saymak?"

Jinx's career flashed before her eyes.

"I left her where I found her," said Bel, and said no more. Honest people may have nothing to fear in an honest court, but smart people don't tell everything they know.

"She's in hiding," said Pel Darzin. "She'll come out, as soon as she knows it's safe."

"In hiding where?" Resa Stelissto stuck to the point with the tenacity of a well-tied ribbon. "That's the question. Where is she? Now?"

"She's on the ship!" Morgan tugged at his chains. "On the ship, or I'm a monkey!"

"The two," Bel began, "are not mutually—"

"Is this true, Captain Joan A. Fazzaria?"

Jinx released her stranglehold on a cucumber sandwich and wiped her hands.

"Yes," said the Captain, giddy with the relief only sudden fatalism can produce. "She's in good health and spirits, as the Ship's Physician, here, can testify. She's been aboard since just after Professor Schuster left the Inn."

"We would like to hear this from the woman, herself," said the Archon.

"Yes, of course." Jinx activated her squawkbox and called for Freldt's transfer to the hall just outside the courtroom.

The Usher showed Freldt in. She still wore Bel's black Capri pants and flowered jersey, but she also wore a gold diamond-cut necklace Bel recognized as her own.

Formerly her own. Bel had lost the necklace to Stefan Batista in Dr. Asimov's Annual Dirty Limerick Contest.

"I see Batista's been teaching you poker," Bel said.

"Yes." Freldt explained to her countrymen, "Funny game. You play for a while, then you scream and tear the cards with your teeth."

"Much as I hate to interrupt," said the Archon, "I seem to find it necessary. Bookkeeper Freldt Saymak?"

"Yes, Mercy."

"Were you approached by an agent of the Galactic Union, and did she change places with you, and were you taken aboard the Galactic Union ship for your safety's sake, and have they treated you nicely?"

"Yes, Mercy. I saw the most wonderful movie; deeply tragic, but uplifting, overall."

"Tell me about it after court. Sergeant Polly, Usher Roderick, remove the prisoners. Court is adjourned. Everyone not in shackles is free to go."

Morgan was rolled from the room with a moan and a rattle of chains that would've done credit to Marley's ghost.

Chapter 32

Jok'rel's Traveler's Rest Inn had never been merrier. The shore party returned, its number swelled by Captain Joan A. Fazzaria, Dr. Vlador Frazni, and Quatro Petrie. The absence of Wotan Hessaphess was noted, but unlamented. The floor show, a twirlpiper and belly-dancer duo, drew enthusiastic applause, and the Galactic Union bought the drinks.

~*~

Gord Pron and Utrop Ligniss saw Gunjin Boktu Jippir onto a deportation transport and returned to the Jipp Joint. Pron swaggered to the office door, making mental notes of the changes in decor and policy he intended to implement. He'd need a new chief bouncer, he reflected, since he planned a different function for Korp Norstu.

The office door was locked.

Pron rattled the knob.

He heard the disengagement buzz, and opened the door. Korp Norstu sat behind the Gunjin's desk, a smoking scentpot in one hand, a hyperlight zip gun in the other.

"Hello, there," she said.

"Hello," said Pron, "uh, boss."

~*~

Connell Morgan looked upon his companion in the barred transport vehicle with a disgust that amounted to absolute detestation. "What do you have to sing about?"

"Do cheer up," said former Councilor Kalator Ganev. "After all, it isn't as if we're going to the Wanderers as common know-nothings, doomed to a life of washing brightly-colored kerchiefs and waxing violins. I know people out here, lad. With your talent and my connections, we'll be elders inside three months, taking our percents from our own pitiful convicts. I have one acquaintance, in particular, who can make things very easy on us. Name of Jack. Jack Foy."

"Ernest in town," said Morgan, wondering if a man could hang himself with a brightly-colored kerchief, "and Jack in the country."

~*~

Bel returned to the ship loaded with souvenirs, tradeables, and the cutest little alley jammer you ever saw. She named him Rosy Joe.

Commissariat Faline Mahoud's matter converter had an accident, and Bel showed up in front of class one day in a new pair of stylish half-boots.

Jinx requested transfer to another post for herself or for Isobel Enid Schuster, she didn't care which.

Neither came through.

About the Author

Marian Allen was born in Louisville, Kentucky and now lives in rural Indiana. For as long as she can remember, she's loved telling and being told stories. When, at the age of about six, she was informed that somebody got paid for writing all those books and movies and television shows, she abandoned her previous ambition (beachcomber), and became a writer.

She's worked as a high school teacher, an executive secretary, a soda jerk, a bank clerk, an accountant, and in Red Cross Youth Services.

She likes connecting and reconnecting with people, meeting new friends and keeping in touch with the friends she already has.

Her writing reflects her love of network. In her books and stories, no one exists in total isolation, but in a web of connections to family, friends, colleagues, self at former stages of maturity, perceptions, and self-images. Most of her work is fantasy, science fiction and/or mystery, though she writes horror, humor, romance, mainstream, or anything else that suits the story and characters.

If you enjoyed this book, please consider buying other titles by this author. Excerpts, blog posts, free stories, and buy links to various formats are available at:

Marian Allen, Author Lady - Fantasies, mysteries, comedies, recipes
http://MarianAllen.com

www.ingramcontent.com/pod-product-compliance
Lightning Source LLC
Chambersburg PA
CBHW071431260626
47170CB00008B/2674